Inspired By

...

2015 tales from

Writers Anthology Group

Of Moreton Bay Region

And other areas of Australia.

Illustrated by

Artists of

Pine Rivers U3A

INSPIRED BY . . .

First published in 2015 by Bent Banana Books in association with the Writers' Anthology Group.

24 Lorraine Court Lawnton, Australia, 4501. 617 3889 2118

Phone 617 3264 2311 Email matt@petercampbellrealty.com

Web www.petercampbellrealty.com

A CiP catalogue record for this book is available from the Australian National Library. ISBN 978-0-9925934-7-6

Cover graphic and design by Ken Armstrong

INSPIRED BY . . .

is dedicated to the memory of Peter Campbell of Albany Creek.

Table of Contents

ToC continued

ToC continued

FOREWORD BY BERNIE DOWLING

ON behalf of the Writers Anthology Group, based in Pine Rivers, Australia, I present our 2015 anthology, *Inspired By* . . . . This is the sixth anthology in the series begun by the Arts Alliance Pine Rivers.

Again we have short stories and poetry illustrated by local artists.

In 2015, we are privileged to have contributions from artists of the Pine Rivers U3A advanced class tutored by Lillian Tebesceff. Check out their excellent illustrations of our authors' literary works.

Some writers, illustrators and editors have been with us from volume one; others are newbies; we thank all for their contributions.

Authors range from people who earn or have earned a living from writing to those being published for the first time.

We include four stories from winners in the Peter Campbell Memorial / WAG Literary Awards for local high school students. Valued anthology sponsor Peter Campbell passed away last year not long after the inaugural awards. Vale Peter; this year's anthology is dedicated to you

Inspired By . . . brings together a diversity of short stories and poetry inspired by literary classics or authors' peculiar interests.

It is always fascinating to see how each year brings a different flavour to our anthology. This year many writers independently chose to render mystery or adventure tales. Add spices of humour, fantasy and drama and you have a literary feast.

We acknowledge the work of our editorial panel: Bernie Dowling, Anne Olsson, Ronald Holt and David MacLaughlin, as well as that of our cover designer/ illustrator Ken Armstrong. We warmly thank our corporate sponsors, the Campbell family of Peter Campbell Realty, based at Albany Creek, and Bent Banana Books of Lawnton.

Now, let the feast begin.

– Bernie Dowling, WAG editorial committee

WRITERS ANTHOLOGY GROUP

WAG was formed following the excellent work done by the Arts Alliance of Pine Rivers in publishing the anthologies:
* *Sweet and Sour*, 2012,
* *Can you believe it . . .* , 2011,
* *The Writing on the Wall*, 2010.

In 2013, WAG published *Serendipity* and in 2014 the fifth anthology *Alpha and Omega* another exceptional publication for local authors and poets.

The Mission of the Writers Anthology Group (WAG) formed in 2013 is to provide pro-bono editorial and administrative support to publish local authors, including unpublished writers.

We are not a traditional writers' group but we work with such groups, libraries and schools to render our mission.

In 2014, WAG and sponsor, the late Peter Campbell, introduced literary awards for local high school students. Albany Creek businessman Mr Campbell presented the inaugural awards.

His family, represented by Peter's son Matt, continues his father's legacy with the WAG Peter Campbell Memorial Award and sponsorship of this anthology.

After the success of Dakabin State High in last year's awards, Pine Rivers State High School scooped the pool this year with Kate Tomsett taking Gold and carving her name to the perpetual trophy.

Fellow PRSHS students Jaidyn Griffin, Caitlyn Heathwood and Mikael Koch received Silver or Bronze medals. We commend their stories during this 100th anniversary of the ill-fated Anzac landing at Gallipoli during World War I.

– Bernie Dowling (WAG editorial committee)

Email bentbananabooks@gmail.com

THE DEADLY DOTTED LINE

Jaidyn Griffin

I FIGHT back the tears with as much might as I can muster. I let my eyes glaze over, as if savoring the sight before me, fearful of his disappearing. I know that the news is coming; I know that the decision has been made but still I won't accept it.

'I've volunteered, Mum,' he says.

My face loses its peachy shade. My lips quiver; my eyes widen; my knees buckle. I pull him into my arms and squeeze as tight as my fragile body will allow. It's only a matter of time until I've lost him. For now, he's here, he's mine and no one else's.

'I start training on Monday,' he says staring into my emerald eyes, triggering another outburst of my tears.

I push him to arms' length, both hands firmly resting on his shoulders. With my lower lip shaking, I stare. I stare into his auburn eyes that so vividly resemble his father's. I stare into his cheeks that will soon be covered with another man's blood. I stare into his mouth that will surely soon report another casualty.

'Why? What possessed you to put yourself in this situation?' I exclaim, swallowing a salted tear. 'Watching the dead, the dying and the soon-to-be in Vietnam has plagued us. We've seen grown men broken. We've seen innocent lives taken at a moment's notice. We've seen the devastation that has been caused, but still, you want to fight?'

'Mum, since I was so young, you have drilled into me the mission of 'facing my fears'. For a long while, I haven't known what those fears were. It could have been heights. It could have been spiders — hey, it could've even been the dark. But what's scarier than all of that put together? Ending another man's life.'

'But . . .'

'Mum, there is nothing scarier, and possibly more rewarding, than ending another man's life who is attempting to end your own.'

My tears stopped flowing. My lip shake had faded. Forever, I had thought that all I saw before me was my innocent little boy. Now I see a man more determined than ever before. And it scares me.

I move the conversation into the kitchen and let a cup of tea diffuse the tension between myself and my son.

'Your father would be so proud of you,' I say with a soft grin, 'He would be proud of who you are, what you've done, and. . . .

'And what, Mum? What *have* I done? I struggle to sleep at night knowing how terrified Dad was in Papua New Guinea. I struggle to do anything productive during my day, because all that's in my mind is just imagining the look of Dad's face when a Japanese bullet tunnelled through his head. If *that's* something to be proud of, well...'

My son's eyes fail to meet mine. We're sitting inches from each other, but never have I felt so distant from him.

'He was petrified,' I begin, 'All your father said in his letters were tales of his mates dying; his body shaking; his passion to live fading.'

'Mum, I know what you're trying . . .'

'Hear me out. The day before his name was called, we had a conversation. He kept talking about how bad the war would be, how committed you had to be to fight. Basically how incompetent he was for the job. A day later, he received the letter. I can still remember those words that changed it all.'

> *Dear Sir,*
>
> *I am writing to inform you, in relation to your liability to call up for national service, that you are required in accordance with the provisions of the CITIZENS MILITARY FORCES ACT to submit yourself to a medical examination prior to commencing your service next month.*

'It was then I knew I had lost him,' I say.

My soon-to-be soldier moves back in his seat, walks over and hugs me from behind. I feel the heaviness of his breath on my neck; I feel the wall he so defiantly formed between us start to crumble.

'What was he like when he read the letter?' asks my son with much curiosity.

'Well...' I begin.

An hour of conversation later, I leave the table and tip my cold, half-full tea down the drain. I think I have succeeded; that my boy is staying and withdrawing his signature from the volunteer form.

When I turn back, I see that I couldn't have been more wrong.

'Thank you for everything, Mum. Really, thank you. But I need to do this; I need to fight in Vietnam.'

There's nothing more I can do. There's no hope.

My son pulls out a thick crimson envelope, almost splitting. He skims over the military jargon and pulls out a form titled 'CITIZENS MILITARY FORCES ENLISTMENT'. Against the sound of my endless sobbing, he clicks the tip of a pen.

'Don't do it,' I manage to say, struggling to breathe, struggling to hold onto my son.

He signs with a quick flick of black ink on the page.

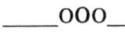

I WALK into church like I normally would on a Sunday. I take a seat, this time front row, to the left of the centre aisle. My heart is pounding. My brain can't slow down. I'm struggling to balance the creased paper between my thumb and forefinger. All this is overshadowed by the well-wishers and support that surrounds me. Father Brian begins the service.

Tall, stiff men in khaki speak of my son. They say he was a courageous young man with everything to live for. They say that he was

11

talented; that his actions were to be applauded. They say that I should be proud of my hero.

I am gestured to take to the podium. A deep breath follows and I manage to steady myself for what lies ahead. I unfold my paper. 'Ladies and Gentlemen, my son *was* courageous.

'When he told me — only 18 months ago — that he had signed up for this war, I used every ounce of my being to make him change his mind – but he didn't.

'He was courageous in the fact that he was determined enough to do what he thought was right.' I pull out a handful of envelopes from my handbag. 'But when he touched-down in Vietnam, all of that courage went flying out the window.'

I look directly at the men who preceded me at the lectern, now standing to the side. 'How *dare* you say that he was talented? How dare you say that his *actions* were to be applauded?

'Because according to these letters — unseen by the Australian Military — my son never fired a single shot. My son never ended, or hindered for that matter, another being's life for the entirety of his Vietnamese campaign.'

The men in khaki look shaken.

I continue with my voice now breaking. 'Many of you may know that my husband fought in Papua New Guinea during World War II. He was forced to fight against his will; forced to fight alongside his mates being killed, one after the other; forced to fight with the Australian Defence Forces. His life was taken by a Japanese bullet. Due to his forced-service, my son wanted to finish the job.'

I walk away from the lectern with my hands shaking and my mouth dry. I sit down in my polished seat and let myself catch my breath. All the things I could have said flood my headspace; all the things I could have done take over my previous thoughts.

Only then do I realise: *I couldn't have done any more than I did. I couldn't have said anything else.*

My son loved me, and he loved his father. His motivation outweighed my persistence. With everything in mind, my son still insisted on signing that godforsaken, deadly, dotted line . . .

. . . *for us.*

INSPIRED BY *Speaking: The Hero* by Felix Pollak

THE GIFT OF NOW
Anne Olsson

Give yourself a gift of love,
Give yourself the gift of Life.
See beyond the world of stress,
Seek the calm beyond the strife.
Let not the mind rob you of peace,
Question not the why or how.
Dwell not in a past or future time,
Be present in this moment now.

Many know not how to live,
And they know not who they are.
They work and strive, they eat and sleep.
They wallow deep and wander far.
The thoughts they think breed discontent,
They question, judge and disallow.
They live in the past or a future time,
But are not present here and now.

Caress the arm of one you love,
Feel the breeze, observe a flower.
Feel the sunlight on your brow,
Hug a tree and feel its power.
Let not the mind rob you of peace,
Think not on who and why and how.
Dwell not in a past or a future time.
Be present here, and present now.

CHANGE THE PICTURE

Belinda Janz

I FIRST met Lilly Bow when she came to my twenty-third birthday party. I had decided to have a pyjama party after seeing a silky little negligée on sale in a Mother's Day catalogue. I took one look at it and thought, *What sort of Mum would wear that?* Certainly not mine.

I was a flirt like so many of my girlfriends back then. I would not have admitted to being a big tease but looking back that is all it was; teasing to get attention.

Lilly was different; younger, blonde hair and blue eyes. At eighteen she seemed to have an air of confidence about her; like she did not care, though this would prove to be supported by medication. She arrived that night in a neck to knee Granny flannelette nightdress with her hair done up in large rollers and a big pink bow on one side. The bow aside, the sight was like looking at my Mother only much younger. Mum wore gowns like that in winter but then she was forty-five.

I sensed in Lilly a gracious and willing nature as she passed a beautiful bunch of fresh flowers across to me accompanied with a smile. Her two housemates stumbled in behind her giggling before they lifted their open cans of beer with cheers towards me. Lilly saw my brother and she gently moved over closer and mouthed a hello above the music. They were attracted to each other; it was obvious but as the night wore on; I found myself attracted to her too. She disappeared at one stage to my brother Michael's concern. It was then that I learnt that Lilly was on some sort of heavy medication to help relieve some issues from her past. Michael enlisted me to help him look for her.

On the corner of the street we found her dancing lightly on tippy-toes around a neighbour's front shrubs as if she had ballet steps to practice. It looked so cute and innocent so we just stood and watched her. A car sped around the corner and the squealing of the brakes snapped Lilly out of the trance. She slipped and stepped in a stagger backwards onto the road. Another car was approaching and just as we heard the second screeching of tyres she righted her step enough to step forward back off the road. She narrowly missed getting hit that night as the second car raced off perhaps chasing the first.

By the time we stepped across to her she was starting to pass out in a faint. Michael grabbed her and between the two of us we guided her back to our house. Michael wanted to put her in my room to sleep as he thought it was just the medication making her so careless. She would be safer sleeping than out drinking with the other party revellers.

About ten minutes later, I decided to check on her. She seemed to be out dead cold. Angus, her housemates and one of Michael's friends, had entered the room behind me after coming out of the loo. He saw Lilly lying flat out on the bed and not realizing the situation threw himself down beside her, leaned over and kissed her full on the lips. She did not respond which surprised me. In fact I was now getting a little worried and so I decided to feel her pulse. I could not find any sign of a beat. By this time a couple of other guests had come into the room to see what was going on. They too tried to find a pulse. Nothing. We just looked at each other as I relayed what had happened earlier. It seemed to sober Angus up somewhat when he realized things could be of a serious nature. He had just started to sit up when Michael walked into the room. He looked at Angus sprawled on the bed. Without a word being uttered Angus climbed quietly off the bed and retreated from the room. It was then Lilly spoke.

Her eyes were still closed but she asked, 'Why am I in jail?'

Michael knelt beside her in the semi dark room and taking her hand had said, 'You are not in jail. You are here with us at Tammy's birthday party.'

'But there are bars all around me. Why am I in jail?' Lilly repeated.

Michael stood up and replied, 'Look no jail, no bars just curtains in Tammy's bedroom.'

He reached across and pulled the heavy curtains open a little way to reveal a large row of white metal pieces that displayed what appeared to be a grill across the window.

'Oh I forgot to tell you Michael, the Landlord finally put some security on our back rooms,' was all I could say as I stared down at Lilly wondering what had triggered that response from her. Surely there was no way she could have known about the new grilles – even Michael did not know that.

At the time I remember thinking her drugs were better than mine if she could trip out like that. Lilly then decided to wash up the dishes ignoring my protest that it was not needed. She put out the cat food for nibbles. Even more strange was watching my friends gobbling up the little dry salmon flavoured pellets like they were an exquisite delicacy. I had sobered up somewhat but they seemed to be driven by the munchy monster to eat like they had just discovered good food.

The next day I checked on her and she appeared sleepy like she had not even gone to bed. I tried to ask her about the pills the doctor had given her. All she could say was that they were for her headaches and that she should not drink alcohol while taking them.

On the Saturday, I had called around to catch up with Lilly at her place and see if she wanted to go somewhere. I knew she did not drive but given the state of stupor she seemed to be in Saturday, I was glad she did not own a car to drive. She seemed semi-unconscious and delirious almost. Her housemate Angie told me that the day before she had stepped out in front of a car while they had been out shopping. It was like she had lost all sense of danger and what was going on around her. Not a care in the world and to make matters worse, their housemate Angus had come home last night and had stumbled into her room drunk.

He had woken Angie as he slammed the front door open falling on the top step into the front room. By the time she had got up to see what was going on she had found the front door wide open and no-one there. Thinking it may have been Lilly off sleep-walking again, she went into

Lilly's bedroom to check on her. There she was passed out from the drugs while Angus lay on top of her massaging inside her open pyjama top over her breasts.

Angie heard him say, 'I could just eat you all up you know and you know you want me.'

Angie said when she had yelled at him, he had simply kissed Lilly on the lips and without saying anything had got up and walked straight out to the kitchen. He was back a moment later with a glass of water which he had thrown over Lilly who was still completely passed out. Angie said she had spent the night curled up next to Lilly in case Angus decided to revisit.

After that Lilly had thrown the pills down the toilet flushing away the fog she had lived in for some months.

One of Michael's mates Jason moved into her life and into her bed. He took over the control in a different way to the pills. He directed her with what he expected and she willingly followed along with everything; living off his every demand. She had briefly confided their first intimate moment had left her scared she would fall pregnant. Jason had promised not to enter her, knowing she was not on birth control and was not yet sexually active. She had trusted him but in a moment of weakness he slipped and suddenly penetration had occurred. Of course he had profusely apologized and had spent time trying to reassure her that he loved her and all would be fine. All was fine; she loved him and that was that. No more was said about the violation I knew Jason had got away with.

Not long after that I took an interstate job transfer; I heard no more from Lilly herself.

About a year later in a phone call from Michael, he mentioned that Lilly and Jason had eventually married. He had not gone to the wedding and that seemed that.

When I had turned up to do a sky dive yesterday, I was more than surprised to see Lilly there with her sister. It had been almost twelve years since I had last spoken to her and yet it was just like yesterday. I noticed straight away she was not wearing her trademark hair bows – gone was the naïve young girl I had once known.

She had finally moved on from Jason. It took Lilly six years to come to that decision after he had an affair with a previous girlfriend. She stayed to please as only she knew how. Still it had not changed things. Jason could still find time in his busy working day to check in with the old girlfriend as she had not handled their affair ending he had said. He never thought she needed his support through the emotional mess.

One afternoon while Jason was off checking on the girl he had strayed with, she met a man in the waiting room of her psychologist. He had made her laugh for the first time in years. It was like a spell had been broken. It took a complete stranger in an innocent moment to make her smile and laugh. Perhaps that was when the realisation really hit home as to what the psychologist had been saying all along. It was time to move on and she did not need Jason to do that or his approval. After that, baby steps became giant leaps including a jump out of a plane.

After the second jump, Lilly told me that her psychologist had said she was caught up in a Red Riding Hood Syndrome of sorts and that she needed to change the picture. Either that or she would remain eaten up in someone else's dreams and aspirations. She discovered she didn't know what she wanted or what she was capable of achieving. Lilly was too afraid to find herself without Jason. She had forgiven him in her goodness all the while not understanding the meaning of true love.

The night before the jump her Dad had said that she would never do it – she would be too afraid to jump when it came down to it. But she had jumped and not only in a tandem but a second time on her own.

Lilly had also confided to me afterwards that she had trusted the guy who took her out on the tandem jump completely. However after the half day training to prepare for the solo jump, she suddenly realized that this jump was the more important of the two.

The Gift Of Love

Sandra Healy

Now she was really afraid – not of dying but of finding out that she did not trust herself to be capable to do the task at hand. She could trust a complete stranger with her life but she had no faith in herself to do right by herself.

That seemed to be a big movement forward for Lilly – the realization that she trusted others with her life but not herself. Throughout life it seemed she had often trusted the wrong person and this had compounded to the point she had lost faith in herself. Even after she made the jump she had briefly spoken of Jason and I knew she had not fully let that wolf go.

Lilly had made plans before the sky dive to take a holiday overseas on her own. When she had been little she had always wanted to travel to Egypt to see the pyramids but Jason had squashed all ideas of overseas travel with fearful notions of being robbed, attacked or worse.

I could see a new picture forming through the cracks; the old Lilly was falling away to a time gone by.

THIS STORY in part parallels a children's story read to me when I was a little girl. The illustrated book was titled *Little Riding Hood* by Brothers Grimm. It was a later edition where the story was tamed down with the grandmother and Little Red Riding Hood being saved.
– Belinda Janz

" SPRING "   Inspired by Vivaldi " Four seasons "

The sweet breath of spring
Has embraced many things.
The dazzling flowers, the nesting birds,
The new soft green of nature
And man heart that sing…

It's sing a song of thanks to HIM
The greatest above it all,
The Lord and Spirit of our souls.

The eternal party has began,
Will you join in the fun?
And the price to all shall be
A new you and a new Me.

Lillian E.Tebesceff (L. Ves-Te

'Look Mummy! When they shoot those fireworks way up high in the sky, they look like pairs of angels' wings made of light when they sideways burst apart.'

ANGELS IN FLIGHT
Vera Murray

Fireworks exploding by man's hand,
Blasting an opening in our sky;
Smashing a door in heaven's shield;
To consume our body's vision,
As we look up, and silently applaud.

Visible now to us earthlings,
In blasts of brightness and sound,
Flapping angel wings are seen,
Giving an unrecognised insight,
Into a world of heavenly light.

Glued to this far off vision,
We wait and keep watch,
To see each pair of wings,
Vanish from our view;
Back in God's invisible world.

INSPIRED BY a child's view of fireworks at the annual Pine Rivers Show.

HULLO RUBY TUESDAY

Bernie Dowling

Hendra, Brisbane, 7.15am, September 17, 1994.

A LARGE shadow passed across the outside of the opaque window but I heard no corresponding crunch on the gravel beneath the sill.

I was enjoying a cuppa of lemongrass tea and, for no particular reason, staring into my lounge where the window was above my two-seater couch.

The knob of the back door turned. The man who entered was tall, about 6ft 6in or whatever that is in centimetres, which is how we officially measure big blokes in Australia.

His gun was a lot smaller, a redundant police .38, which, unless they passed a law while I slept, was unlawful in a private hand.

I put down my teacup and raised my hands.

He waved the gun at me. 'Don't be fucking stupid.' He put the gun in the pocket of his suit coat. 'I didn't know if you'd still be here, Steele.'

I put my hands down. 'I thought the unlocked back door would have given it away. Long time no see, Ruby.'

He rubbed a knuckle of his closed right hand against the stubble on his chin. Discoloured puffy skin under his eyes and a crumbled grey suit were signs of a man who had slept rough for days. 'Five years, more than five years since I seen ya last, Steele.'

'Whereya bin, Ruby?'

'Running a business in Thailand.'

'Business good?'

'Yair, good.'

Actually, in 1989, Ruby Tuesday was one of the first invited guests of the new Sir David Longland Correctional Centre; the nick with a knighthood, we called it. It was a max-sec prison in the outer Brisbane suburb of Wacol so we felt sorry for the relatively gentle giant bunking

26

down with some dangerous types. Not sorry enough to support him at his trial or visit him in prison. In our book such endeavours would surely lead to Ruby's bad luck rubbing off.

The judge gave him seven large for embezzlement. This seemed a harsh judgement as Ruby's employer was a bank, hardly the most reputable of institutions. The prosecution said Ruby stole 800k, but our punting crowd didn't recall the then 28-year old, flashing that sort of money about in 1989. Maybe he used the bugs-bunny to buy his sweetheart a 7-carrot diamond ring, ha-ha. Ruby kept banging on about this 'sensational chick' he had met.

Oh yair, the name Ruby Tuesday, almost forgot. Honestly I couldn't tell you his real name. None of us could. All we ever called him for years was Ruby. I was the first to do it and it stuck.

He had this chunk of a ruby set in a silver ring. If the ring was not on the customary finger, you knew he was going bad on the punt. In those days the big metropolitan race meeting of the week was on the Saturday and the big provincial meet was on the Wednesday. I was barred from all Australian racetracks for life by then but a few of us would meet in a pub near the track of the day an hour or so before the first race. One Wednesday morning he arrived ringless at the Racehorse Hotel Booval. I asked him if he'd been to the pawnshop that morning and he said, yesterday. 'Goodbye Ruby Tuesday,' I said. He has been Ruby Tuesday ever since.

Five years later, it was hullo Ruby Tuesday; tell me some fibs about your business in Thailand. I put on the coffees and invited him to take a seat beside me at the small kitchen table. He looked warily to gauge the strength of the wooden chair I offered before I convinced him it was one of the Salvos' Op Shop's finest.

Despite the warm morning he took a large swig of hot coffee and produced a manila envelope from a coat pocket with his free hand. The envelope thudded on to the tabletop. 'There's 25 hundred there,' Ruby said. 'Another 25 when you find her.'

'Find who?'

'Lucretia.'

'Who's she? Why me?'

'I always thought you were the smartest of our bunch, smarter than that accountant, that lawyer even.'

'That wouldn't be hard. That lawyer, your defence lawyer, watched you go down for seven years.'

'What are you talking about, Steele?'

'Sorry Ruby, forgot about Thailand.'

'She promised not to say anything to you mob about it.'

'She didn't, it was in the paper.'

He raised his shoulders. 'Anyway Grace did a good job. She found out later the judge had shares in my bank.'

'Is that appealable?'

'Apparently not. Anyway that is all behind me. Lucretia and I will settle down now. Might even open a tourist restaurant in Thailand, for real.'

'Sounds like making customized number plates in prison pays well.'

'Maybe I made some lucrative investments which were not traced. Maybe I had more money than people thought. Maybe I won big on the horses.'

'If I'm supposed to guess which of the above happened I am eliminating a big win on the ponies.'

Ruby erupted in laughter and you could see some of the tension fall from his face. 'Other things I like about you, Steele, are you're funny and not greedy. You won't turn me in.'

'Every punter's greedy, Ruby. You on the run?'

'Nah, I done me time. Just keeping a low profile, that's all.'

I done me time. I looked up at Ruby. His grammar had nosedived in the nick and his once handsome face looked closer to 40 than 30. He could use a decent break. I could use $2500.

'Tell me about Lucretia.'

'You know the Cotton Candy Club?'

I nodded.

'She worked there.'

'A stripper in a strip joint.'

'An exotic dancer in a gentlemen's club. Lucretia called it performance art.'

You don't laugh in the face of a sleep-deprived giant who has handed you $2500. You try really hard not to and you don't. 'Did Lucretia go to your trial and visit you at Sir David Longland?'

'I asked her not to. I had given her a bit of money and I did not want the cops to find out about her and me.'

'How much is a bit of money?'

Ruby hesitated and cast down his eyes before he answered softly. 'Ten grand.'

I picked up the envelope with the dough inside and passed it between the fingers of each hand. I pushed it towards Ruby but changed my mind and thrust it out of sight into one of the front pockets of my jeans.

Lucretia – her family was More, according to Ruby – wrote to him every week for two years. The letters were always addressed from a Post Office Box in Fortitude Valley. Lucretia told him she had moved a couple of times but only gave her new suburbs, not street names. In one letter, she wrote she was leaving Brisbane but not where she was headed. Only one letter came after that. It was sent December, 1990, almost three years ago.

'Three years can be a long time,' I said. 'Surely you must have thought she's found someone else. What are you gunna do if she is with him now?'

'I dunno. Just find her and we'll worry about that later.'

I didn't much like the sound of that. The old Ruby would walk away if he found Lucetia More – 100 to one that being her real name – in the arms of another. But five years in the nick pining over a lost love could do serious damage to anyone's straight thinking. If I did find Lucretia, I could be partly responsible for Ruby doing her serious damage.

Thankfully the chances were I would never find her but get to keep most of the $2500, even with zero prospects of getting the other 25. That I could live with.

I scribbled down the name and room number of the four-star hotel Ruby was staying in. If he could not get a good night's sleep there, his head space was totally out of whack. I put a photo-booth snap of Lucretia in my wallet. Ruby ate his share, most, of the grilled cheese and tomato on toast I prepared for us and he went on his way.

Grace Istinova was a junior partner in the law firm Hugo Ducking and Weaving. That wasn't the real name of the law firm in Edward St, Brisbane City, within easy walking distance of Central railway station. I had rung Grace beforehand but had not told her what it was about. She offered me a chair in a tiny office with a side view of a big brick wall.

I was sipping on my coffee – milk no sugar – when Grace skipped the preliminaries. She was quite pretty – beautiful even – a descendant of White Russians and she had flawless pale skin and pixie-cropped blonde hair. I can't tell you much about White Russians except the cocktails don't come from Russia and the people do. After two kids, Grace had kept her figure and her terse dialogue. 'Before you start, Steele, I've ditched crim law.'

I pretended to be offended by her implication I might be cadging free legal representation. 'Who, me? I'm not in any trouble, at least not legal wise.'

'So you're still with Natalie, then?'

'Sort of, but this is about a former client of yours, Ruby Tuesday.'

'Tyrone Wells, what about Tyrone? It wasn't my fault, you know.'

Ruby was Tyrone, you learn something new every day. 'So Ruby says, even after doing five of a seven-year sentence. Did you ever meet his girlfriend Lucretia?'

'Meet her, I introduced them. Mary was in a couple of my law classes.'

'Who's Mary?'

'Mary, Mary Moore, M-O-O-R-E, was Lucretia More.'

'When did you see her last?'

'About three years ago. I tried to convince her to go back to finish her law degree after Tyrone went to jail. Stripping's not much of a career.'

'Did she?'

'Said she'd think about it and disappeared off the face of the earth.'

'Talk about disappearing, Grace, we don't see you down the pub anymore before the races.'

'You know how it is, Steele. You get married, a couple of kids, a partnership and your God-given vocation to punt on racehorses goes out the window.'

'Life's tough,' I said.

Grace came over to my seat and bent down to kiss me on the cheek. 'I'm hearing you brother,' she said before she showed me to the door.

The Cotton Candy Club opens at 8pm on a Saturday and I was waiting at the door at 10-to. This would be my first attempt to earn Ruby's money the hard way. The funny thing about a gentleman's club is neither the owner nor the patrons are gentlemen. If I started to ask questions at 3am I would be looking at the club fist of a 7ft bouncer. At 8pm I might get away with just being told to fuck off. Ah well, you gotta try.

I had the feeling of being watched and looked carefully around. Looking back at the big metal door, I saw a peep hole just below my head.

'What the hell are you doing here?' The voice came from beside the Besser-block right wall. I knew that voice. Beautiful blonde hustler Crystal Speares stepped out into the night. 'Get your ass around here, Steele. We can't have choir boys like you raising the tone of the place.'

'You stripping now, Crystal?'

'These losers can't afford me. I manage the joint whenever I need some play money. And let me guess, you're here on some Boys-Brigade adventure rather than for a perve.'

'Can we talk?'

She shook her head but walked behind the building to open the back door to show me into a tiny room. She indicated a chair to the side of a desk which she sat behind so she could look into the club through a large two-way mirror. She reached for a cigarette and gold lighter.

'Those fags'll kill you, Crystal.'

'Yair, but hanging around with you is quicker. Waddya want, Steele, and the answer's *no*.'

'I need to speak to a couple of the girls.'

'It's been nice, Steele. The answer's *no*.'

'Come on Crystal. The woman I am looking for hasn't worked here for three years. No harm done to you or the club if I get a lead.'

She considered that. 'Why not? I can always tell everyone at your funeral I was kind to you once.'

'The people in our retirement village won't believe you.'

She laughed. We left the office to arrive at another door Crystal knocked on. 'Are you decent? Crazy man to see you, he's not a cop.'

The door opened to reveal five women in various stages of undress.

The redhead who opened the door was naked. 'I'm wearing my work clothes,' she said.

Crystal grabbed the other side of the door knob. 'Hurry up, we open in half an hour.'

'The sign says 8pm opening, not 8.30,' I reminded her.

'Aw, gee,' she tittered. 'Our secret shoppers are gunna mark us down. You got 10 minutes, Steele.' She shut the door as I squeezed past.

'Any of you girls working here three years ago?' I asked.

Two blondes put up their hands. When I said the name Mary Moore, one remained expressionless and the other dropped her eyes. I asked to speak to the eye-dropper outside. She grabbed a purse from the top of a dresser and followed me to the club floor.

Madonna Starr – double n, double r; she said – was her name. It didn't matter whether it was real. She was about 5'10, under 30 and looked like she had her breasts, eyes and lips done. You would hope she would be able to claim the ops on her tax. At first she answered my questions in monosyllables but my charm eventually broke through.

'Mary was my best friend. We started the same night here.'

I told Madonna nothing had happened to Mary though I was far from sure about that.

'You couldn't separate us. Then she changed. Too tired to hang with me during the day, she said. Thought I didn't notice the thousand-dollar dresses she was starting to wear to work sometimes. The worst thing was she could have told me. Instead she just went and disappeared. She could have told me. You know what I mean.'

'I think I do.'

Madonna reached into her purse and produced a club business card. She flipped it over to reveal a mobile phone number.

'You got a pen,' I asked.

'Keep the card,' she said and walked back into the dressing room.

I passed the front door of the Cotton Candy Club on the way back to my car. Again feeling watched I looked around at the dozen men waiting patiently to enter. I waved in the direction of the peep hole.

Mary Magdalinos answered the mobile. *Magdalinos* – where did I know that name? I said I had an important message from an old friend, Tyrone Wells. *What's the message?* Sorry Mary, I can't tell you over the phone. Where can we meet? *That's impossible. I can't meet up with a stranger. How'd you get my number, anyway?* Madonna Starr gave it to me. If it helps, I can bring Grace Istinova with me to meet you.

I was dropping names faster than a tryhard on a first date and I hoped one of them impressed Mary.

You sure Tyrone won't be with you?

Positive.

She gave me an address at Surfer's Paradise on the Gold Coast.

There's a double gate on your left and a smaller gate to the right of the house. Come exactly at 10am, tomorrow, and I will open the gate on the right for you. Drive down to the end and you will see me by the canal. Don't bother Grace. Come alone, um, er, I don't even know your name.

It's Steele.

Like iron and steel.

Something like that. See you at 10 tomorrow.

I pulled up beside the squillion-dollar mansion and parked the red EH ute in front of the double gates to frighten the neighbours. They could probably see the car with the very strong binoculars they needed for grouse shooting from their side veranda. As Fate would have it, I had been in some swanky houses but the sight of one up close still gave me the creeps. Nat calls it my inverse snobbery and she is probably right. Don't tell her I said that.

The smaller gate to the right of the mansion opened as if by magic to reveal the canal in the distance. I trekked down the private bitumen road and heard the metal gate clang shut behind me.

Mary stood beside an outdoor table festooned with cakes, sandwiches, bottles of spring water, a jug of juice, a coffee pot, cups and glasses. She was a tall blonde of striking beauty and she wore a Lacoste polo shirt, designer jeans of a label I couldn't see, and red and black Balmain trainers. Her mouth looked as if it did not know whether to smile or sneer and so did a bit of both.

'Good morning Mrs Magdalinos,' I said cheerily. 'How's Mr Magdalinos.'

She seemed wary. They tell me rich people fear kidnapping, a complaint we stock of the common herd do not have, with the possible exception of drug dealers. But I wasn't trying to frighten her. I had just remembered where I knew the name Magdalinos. Alex Magdalinos was one of the biggest property developers on the Gold Coast, the sort of bloke who would live in a mansion on a canal estate.

'Would you like some coffee and morning tea, Steele?'

'Just coffee, thanks, white no sugar.' A shaking hand poured the coffee. 'I'm not here to harm you, Mrs Magdalinos.'

'Alex is fine, on business in China. Please call me Mary.'

'I would except we both know your being Mrs Magdalinos is why I'm here today.'

'Why are you here?'

'I have a client. Ruby, I call him; Tyrone you know him as. Ruby's been a lot in his 33 years. Accountant in a bank, degenerate gambler, embezzler, jailbird, head over heels in love. And now he's my client.'

'How much do you want?'

I looked at her and took a sip of coffee. I decided I might eat after all, two of those small sandwich triangles with the crusts cut off. Egg and lettuce, though I spied tuna and mayo as well as ham and cheese and a few whose contents I was unsure of. 'Blackmail? You think I'm a blackmailer?'

'Just tell me how much you want and go. Please.'

'I'll explain, Mary. With a bit more digging I could have found this address and given it to Ruby. If he were the Ruby Tuesday I knew five years ago, gentle giant and so on, I would have done just that. But jail changed him. Turned him into Tyrone Wells. I don't know what that bloke's likely to do. I decided I'd better see you before I tell Tyrone anything.'

She walked around the table nervously and almost fell into a chair and rested her forehead in her hands before looking up at me. 'Tyrone is a wonderful man. He is gentle and sweet. But he is so blind. He couldn't see that I never loved him.'

I wasn't in the market for this distraught-philosopher bizo. 'You took his ten grand and promised to wait.'

'I haven't touched a cent of that money, I promise. It's been in a term deposit for five years and Tyrone can have it all back with the interest.'

'Why'd you take the money and say you'd wait?'

'Why? Why I did every stupid thing. Why I went stripping when Dad left Mum and she had to bring up four kids. Why I went out with Tyrone when I knew he wasn't my type. Why I didn't go back to uni when Crystal said I was the best, most reliable worker they ever had.'

I nodded. 'Yes, always believe everything the management of a strip joint tells you.'

'Crystal's lovely and she said I could have the manager's job within a few years.'

I wasn't sure in what sense Crystal was lovely. The Crystal I knew was deadly. 'Then why'd you leave?'

'I was partying too hard. Worrying about the future and whether I should go back to law. Go back to Tyrone. The party was endless, day and night – coke, eccies, speed, tequila; not too much smack, thank God. It was starting to mess with my head and my body. And that's when I met Alex. And fell in love.'

'How old's Alex?'

'Forty-six, but it's not what you think. I love him.'

I looked into my empty coffee cup for inspiration. 'Here's what I suggest. You fly to Sydney and send the 10 grand to Ruby. I'll phone with the address as I don't know how long he will be where he is now. You send him a letter with the dough. Tell him what you just told me without any names. No names at all. Most important. Take out a Post Office Box in Sydney and pay some bloke, not a woman, to collect the mail but not often and at night. Write or better still type letters to Ruby. If he sounds like he's together, you might meet him. It's up to you. I can arrange for discreet protection. I am ready to listen to a different plan as long as it does not involve shopping Ruby to the coppers'

'I'll go along with your idea, Steele, but what are you going to say to Tyrone?'

'Tell him I couldn't find you but I had a tip you'd gone interstate. Don't like lying to Ruby, but I gotta play the cards the way I read them.'

She reached for a handbag I hadn't noticed under the table. She unzipped it and I saw a small gun sitting on top of a pile of stuff. Why do so many people I run into carry guns? Didn't their mothers tell them to play nice? Mary picked up the gun. She buried it at the bottom of the bag and grabbed a large envelope to hand to me.

'What's that?'

'Five grand. Isn't that what you call it, Steele, grand, for a thousand dollars. I was sure you were here to blackmail me.'

I chuckled. 'Yair we call it a grand or sometimes a large.' I opened the envelope, took our three 100-dollar bills and handed the rest back to her.

She put the money back in her purse and took out a remote control. 'Opening the gate,' she said. 'Wanna lift to the street?'

I shook my head and pointed my finger towards the canal. 'My mate Gooroo says these canals will flood all your homes, maybe in less than 50 years. Ever heard of the Greenhouse Effect, Mary?'

'No, but I have heard of the Tall Puppy Syndrome. It sounds like a variation on that.'

'Maybe. The Greenhouse Effect is the earth warming. Gooroo says Bangladesh will be almost totally submerged. I don't know if that's tall-poppy stuff, but rising seas dumping on California could be.'

'I don't think any of that will happen in our lifetime, Steele.'

I dropped my hand. 'You're probably right. Bugger the grandkids, that's what I always say.'

Mary, the stripper formerly known as Lucretia, crooked her arm around mine and we walked towards the road.

As we rounded the corner, the silver Honda Civic hurtled towards us. Startled, we both froze. The car braked to stop at the side of the road, five feet from us. Ruby looked comical as he clambered from the small car. None of us laughed.

Ruby was puzzled by Mary's appearance as she was a lot different from the woman in the photo he had given me. Love kicked in and with it recognition. He looked to his left, took in the huge mansion and frowned.

I let go of Mary's arm and moved a pace away from her. 'Hullo, Ruby.'

Mary had an expression you could not read. 'Tyrone, this is my life now. I'm married, trying for kids. I'm sorry, Tyrone.'

The big man shuffled his feet. 'Hi Mary, hi Steele.'

Of course Ruby had known her name was Mary Moore. Why had he given me only her stage name, Lucretia More? A pop psychologist might say he was in love with a fantasy. Me I reckon he thought I would be a better chance of finding her by starting at the Cotton Candy Club. Five years in jail and Ruby was still a punter, playing the odds.

He took the same gun from the same crumpled suit which he'd worn two days earlier. A crooked smile creased his mouth. Ruby turned the .38 towards his heart and managed to pull the trigger. Twice.

Mary reacted quickly while my feet were glued to the bitumen. She put delicate fingers on Ruby's huge wrist and turned her head towards me. 'I think he's gone.'

She stood up and was shaking now. So was I. Blood stained her white Lacoste polo shirt. Mary rushed to the house and returned with a blanket and mobile phone. She placed the blanket over Ruby, keeping his heat visible.

I was angry now. At Ruby and at myself. 'How are you going to explain this, Mary? That was selfish of Ruby.'

She was not having it. 'No Steele. He thought this was the best answer for me and for him. Ruby was a good man.' She had called him Ruby. She recognized him as the gambler who had thrown the dice one last time. 'You'd better go Steele. You could get into trouble when the paramedics call the police.'

Mary or Lucretia, always looking after someone else. Her great gift. Her curse. 'We'll catch up down the track,' I vowed and she nodded.

We never did.

RAYMOND CHANDLER fans will know *Hullo Ruby Tuesday* is inspired by the 1940 novel *Farewell My Lovely*.

THE TIME MAY COME?
Francis E J Beecher

The time may come when thoughts once so easy to my pen will no longer flow,
As memory, so often seemingly a fading gift, forgets, and says I do not know.
Words their meaning to my mind are lost, as my knowing is not of what I do.
How then can I tell you in words of sense, just how filled is my heart of you?

How then could I tell you how much I love you, how much of my life you are?
When in my mind that day I see not you, but see all my memories from afar?
That such a time may come to me, is so likely, this so often I've been told.
It's one of those joys of life to look forward to, when ones bones are growing old?

Yet this heart will never lose its beat, which is of you, your love each day.
No matter just how lost my mind may be, if ever it shall lose its way!
My heart shall never lose your fire, your gift of love to me you see.
As long as this heart beats your love lives, I am you and you are me!

So my darling I take this chance to tell you while today I still may do!
Just how much my whole life is in your hands, as also is my heart, its true!
And just as now in love I rest, knowing of your love's call each day anew.
Forgive and love me as I am, if that day comes, my mind it knows not you!

INSPIRED BY love

THE WEDDING DAY

Anne Olsson

THE lake looked serene in the early morning light. A pelican flew down gracefully, and settled comfortably on the water. A breeze brushed through the trees lining its edge. Layla looked across to the north-west, solemnly watching the last of the fruit bats flying in to their rest in the rookery.

Today was the day of her cousin Judy's wedding, but it was too soon. Her pain was too raw. It was only two weeks – two short weeks – since her brother David had died. Two dark and lonely weeks of confusion and desolation. He was to have been the best man today. Now another man would stand in his place.

Forlorn, she wandered back to the house where preparations were already under-way for the big day. The hairdresser had arrived early to dress the bride's hair. Flowers were waiting to be delivered to St. Joseph's Church. Her aunt Sophie was anxious because the caterers had not yet arrived. Judy came out of the shower, flustered because she was not yet ready to have her hair done. Her uncle Peter was the only family member who seemed unperturbed.

The reception was to be held under a big marque in the garden at the back of the house. The garden overlooked the lake. The marque had been erected, and tables were set up, draped with white linen cloths and decorated with flowers. Layla wandered amongst them, reluctant to be helpful. 'This shouldn't be happening,' she thought. 'Why hadn't they postponed this wedding?' But she had been present when this was discussed. Her Uncle Peter had argued that David would have wanted it to go ahead. Her aunt was concerned that a postponement would be too disruptive. All arrangements for the wedding had been completed, and some family members were coming from interstate and overseas, having organised their flights and time away from their work to come. So Layla had held her tongue, and made no protest.

'Layla!' her aunt entreated her impatiently. 'Will you come and man this video camera?' She came hurrying out into the garden. 'Judy wants the hairdressing to be filmed. You will have time to do her make-up afterwards. And then you must get ready yourself. Time is slipping by.'

The ceremony at the church was due to start at 11 am. It was being conducted by the same minister in the same church in which David's funeral service had been held. How could she bear to see her cousin so happy there, and so soon to forget her grief over David's death? Too soon. Far too soon. She was the only bridesmaid. If only they had found someone to replace her too.

When her tasks were completed, she stood in the bedroom set aside for her, looking at herself in the mirror. She was wearing the beautiful dress that had been specially designed for her for the wedding, but she took no pleasure in her appearance. She gathered together the long tendrils of her blonde hair and arranged them at the nape of her neck. She brushed mascara on her long lashes and gave her lips a final brushing of lipstick.

'Layla,' Judy called to her from her bedroom, 'please come and help me with my dress.' She found Judy in a flurry of excitement, her eyes alight as she held her wedding dress up against her body.

'It is so beautiful! Oh, I am so happy, Layla,' she exclaimed. When she saw the look of consternation upon Layla's face, she was contrite.

'I am sorry, darling girl! I know you are feeling desperately miserable. But I am sure David would have wanted us to get married as we planned. If I doubted this, I wouldn't have gone ahead with it.'

Layla's face was expressionless. What could she say? The wedding was going ahead anyway. No one could ask David what he wanted now.

'How could we ever know what he really wanted?' she mumbled. 'Here, let me help you on with your dress.' She took the beautiful dress gently out of Judy's arms and unzipped the zipper.

'Take off that dress you're wearing, and I'll slip it over your head.'

With the dress snugly fitting the curves of her body, and the veil placed delicately over her hair, Judy looked very pretty. *Well, at least she is happy with her appearance*, thought Layla bemusedly.

She left Judy and ventured downstairs. The caterers had arrived and taken over the kitchen. Her aunt was preparing to leave for the church, fearful that arrangements would be incomplete when the wedding party arrived.

'Did you help Judy with her dress, Layla?' she asked.

'Yes, I did. And she looks beautiful.'

'I will pop up to see her now before I leave. Your uncle is still fussing over which cuff links to wear with his suit.' Layla thought this unlikely, but did not say so. Her aunt left for the church soon afterwards, still in a flurry in case something had been forgotten.

When the bride and her father arrived at the church in a chauffeur-driven limousine, Layla was waiting to walk behind them up the aisle. The music of *the Wedding March* resounded solemnly through the old building.

When Layla had taken up her position to the north side of the transept, she looked across to the anxious face of the groom. Brian was standing nervously, with his hands grasped in front of him, watching Judy intently. Beside him stood the imposing figure of his best man. To Layla's amazement, she recognised him, but this was not the man she was expecting to see there.

Why, it's Simon Finley, she thought. His eyes met hers, and he smiled. Simon had been at school with her brother David. They had been close friends until the end of their school days, when Simon left the town to study at Sydney University. He had come often to their home in those days, and, as a sixteen-year-old, she had been infatuated with him. He had returned for David's funeral, but she had not spoken to him then, and had not seen him since. She was sure he had not been originally invited to the wedding. She could not understand how he came to standing beside the groom as his best man. Had not Simon's brother Alan been chosen to replace David?

As she absently listened to the minister methodically droning the words of the service, Layla was conscious of the heaviness of her heart. Despite her resolution to remain stoic, tears welled in her eyes. She brushed them away, but her grief remained.

'David should be here,' she thought bitterly. She endeavoured to distract her mind by examining the flowers decorating the church. She was caught unawares when the joyful couple embraced fondly and kissed each other shyly.

The minister felicitated the couple on their marriage, and the newly designated husband and wife walked arm-in-arm up the aisle, receiving congratulations from friends and family on both sides of the nave. When the couple prepared to drive away, Judy intentionally tossed her bouquet in the direction of her bridesmaid, and unconsciously Layla caught it. She laughed. Then her sadness rushed to greet her again, and she felt guilty, fearing that in her moment of joy she had betrayed her brother's memory.

When all the guests had gathered in the garden for the reception, photographs of the bridal party were taken. Champagne was served. The caterers brought the first of the three courses to the tables.

Layla was seated quietly in her place beside Judy, and was prepared to smile and make the small talk that she felt was expected of her. The speeches began. When the best man stood to speak and propose a toast to the bride and groom, Layla looked on with curiosity. How well Simon had known Brian, she did not know, but he told amusing stories of Brian's teenage years and of how he first met Judy. His speech was not long, but it was funny and clever.

As the afternoon drew on, Layla began to feel very tired. The strain of continually smiling and maintaining gay conversation was telling on her. As soon as she felt it appropriate she excused herself, and walked down to the lake. The water looked still and cold.

Kate Simonville

She followed the edge of the lake to the west until she came to a track that led through a grove of paper-bark trees. She took the familiar path until she came to a timber cottage nestled amongst the trees. A sigh escaped her. This had been David's home.

It was a small and simple bungalow with only two bedrooms, but the interior was cosy. She found the key under a pot plant on the front porch, and carefully opened the door. She felt her body relax as she walked into the familiar living room. David's presence was evident everywhere. Here were his books and his battered guitar. A well-worn pullover was slung over an armchair. Magazines were scattered on the coffee table. David was speaking to her from every corner of the room.

Tears welled in her eyes as she stepped into his bedroom. A wardrobe door was standing open, revealing a neat rack of his clothes hanging within. The doona on the bed was roughly pulled into place and a book was lying on the bedside table, still open at the last page that he had been reading. But David would not sleep in the bed again, and the book would remain unfinished.

It was the sound of the front door opening that brought Layla out of her reverie. She felt a moment of anxiety until she heard a voice calling to her.

'Layla, are you there?'

When she returned to the hall, she was surprised to see Simon standing there. She felt irritated. She wanted so much to be alone. He had removed his jacket and loosened his tie, but otherwise looked calm and dignified. He was not a handsome man, but he had a presence that commanded attention.

'I'm sorry if I frightened you,' he apologised. 'I hope you don't mind my following you, but I was hoping to speak to you alone.' She looked up at him with impatience, not responding to his words.

'Look, can we find the makings of a cup of tea in the kitchen?' he asked. 'I would love a cup right now.'

'Layla led him into the small kitchen. There was no fresh milk, so without speaking, she boiled the kettle and made them each a cup of black sweet tea.

'You weren't expecting to see me at the wedding, were you?' he suggested. 'Especially not as best man.'

She glanced at him indifferently. 'No,' was her first word to him. 'That was a mystery. But I don't mean to imply that you are not welcome.'

He watched her closely before he spoke. 'I didn't have an opportunity to talk to you at the funeral. You were always surrounded by friends and family. But there is something I need to talk to you about.'

'That was a sad day,' she mused solemnly.

'You know that David and I were close friends at school,' he stated, 'but you may not know that we have been partners in a business together for several years.'

'No, I did not know'. For some reason she did not want to talk to this man about David. Not right now. The wind had arisen, and blew the back door shut. Layla was startled. She got up from her chair nervously and looked out the kitchen window. 'Looks like we're going to get another storm. At least the weather has been fine for the reception.'

'Layla, there is something I need to say to you,' he stressed. 'Something you need to hear.'

She sat down again, but appeared disinterested, distant and non-committal.

'Would you like to know how I came to be at the wedding?' he asked.

'Yes,' was all she said.

'Alan had agreed to take David's place as best man, but three days ago he drove north to Ingham on business. They've had torrential rain up north, and big floods had blocked the roads. He knew he wouldn't get back in time for the wedding. I am not sure he wasn't glad of an excuse to avoid being best man. He'd agreed to it reluctantly. He rang Brian, and suggested that I fill in for him. I have known Brian for years, and the suit fitted me. The jacket is a little tight in the arms but I could wear it. So you see, there is no great mystery.'

They heard the rumble of thunder in the distance.

'I think we should be getting back to the reception. They will wonder where we are,' Layla suggested, watching the clouds building in the west through the window.

'Layla,' Simon spoke impatiently, 'there is something I must say to you.' She met his gaze resignedly. 'David and I were in business together. He didn't want the family to know because it was risky. Very risky. If the venture had failed we would both have been bankrupt.' He looked at her, hoping to see some signs of interest in her face. 'The venture was successful. We both made a lot of money. I mean – a lot of money. I didn't find out the full extent of it until five days ago.'

The rumble of thunder had increased, and a flash of lightning illuminated the darkening room.

Simon's voice became more intense. Layla looked at him now with awakening curiosity.

'I know you miss David dreadfully. I do too. But you need to hear this. Because of the immensity of what we were planning, I insisted that David make a will.' He was quiet for a moment. 'He has left everything to you, Layla. This house, his money, all his shares. You are a very wealthy woman.'

She stood up, bewildered and disbelieving.

'We must get back before the storm hits,' she murmured. Simon did not move.

'Sit down, Layla,' he said firmly. 'David loved you. His little sister was the apple of his eye. He spoke of you often, and told me that if anything happened to him, he wanted you to have everything.'

He reached out and laid his hand upon hers. Layla sank back into her chair, and the protective wall she had so carefully constructed to hide her sorrow came tumbling down. Tears flowed down her cheeks and she sobbed quietly. Simon said nothing more. He held her hand and let her cry. They sat like that together as the darkness of the room deepened, and rain began to fall on the roof. Simon drew a handkerchief from the pocket of his trousers and passed it to her. She accepted it wordlessly. She wiped the tears from her cheeks and blew her nose. When her sobs began to ease, she stood up awkwardly and thanked him.

But we really must go back now,' she whispered. He stood up beside her and drew her into his arms, and gently cradled her. She rested her head upon his shoulder thankfully, trustingly. She did not feel the urgency of returning now. She felt safe. She felt tranquil for the first time since David's death.

'Now I think it is time we set off,' Simon murmured. 'There must be an old brolly around somewhere that we could use.'

She looked up at him unguardedly, and nodded. Searching in the hall cupboard, Simon discovered a dusty umbrella. They set out together into the rain, Simon with his arm around Layla, holding the umbrella over them both. When they arrived back in the garden, there was no one in sight and the tables had been cleared away. They found a group of people talking and laughing, gathered together in the lounge room, but the other guests had already departed.

Layla gave Simon a serene and grateful smile, and asked after Judy. She was told she was upstairs, preparing to leave for the honeymoon. She looked back at Simon affectionately.

'I'm just going up to say goodbye to Judy,' she called to him. 'I won't be long. Please wait for me.'

Layla found Judy alone, sitting reflectively on the bed, stroking the beautiful wedding gown that lay beside her. Layla reached out for her hand and drew her to her feet.

Where did you get to?' Judy queried. Layla hugged her lovingly.

Just went for a walk,' she said. 'I'm sorry if I've been a wet blanket, Judy. I'm so very sorry. I know David would have wanted you to have the happiest of weddings. I'm all right now. I love you, Judy. I hope you have a great time in Bali, and I'll look forward to hearing all about it when you get back.'

She hugged her again. Now there was no resentment and no bitterness. She smiled, because her wishes were wholehearted, and her heart was glad. A rush of joyous excitement arose within her, knowing that Simon was waiting for her below.

INSPIRED BY Rosamunde Pilcher's *Spanish Ladies*.

Prize-winning yellow rose at the Pine Rivers Show.

Sucked into a Vortex
and thrown on new land

THE LAST PROPHECY
Kerry Hall

In times yet to pass; in a world out of reach.
Three Masters of all will sunder a breach.
The test they will fail, the power be too grand,
Sucked into a vortex and thrown on new land.
In time they will Reign, many wars to be fought,
Their bloodlines to mingle and peace will be sought.

When days start to cool, from the very hot sun,
Two souls will be born; instead of just one.
Far in the west, the three blood lines of old
Will converge bright in one; the second behold.

The first will be strong, a friend to the King,
The second will dance the blue flame she will sing.
A struggle to live, her will shall be strong,
Her mantra, her soul will not falter or wrong.
A leader of men, for peace she will fight
The evil that comes and steals in the night.

The ancients of old will know when they see,
The one that is she; to set the world free.
Three gifts she will find, to help with her quest
But to win, play the game, may cleave her heart yet.'

INSPIRED BY- J.R.R Tolkien's *Lord of the Rings*.

NULLARBOR MYSTERY

Ronald Holt

WHAT a year! I've been shot at; king hit twice; crucified by defence barristers; and people wonder why I like being a Queensland detective. It can't be the pay. No one gets enough for all that. Maybe it's the adrenaline rush. No matter what I think, when the wife says that it's time to get away before anything else happens, what can a man do?

Her choice of destination was not my preference. I would have gone to somewhere exotic but it was on the wife's bucket list. Little did I realise that I was about to face a mystery far from home which would test my investigative skills.

My wife has an obsession with flowers and the West Australian wildflower season in September was like a magnet. She wanted to travel on the Indian Pacific train across the Australian continent. Because reservations from Sydney were unavailable, she booked the Perth departure. That meant a six hour flight from Brisbane to Perth. I don't usually sleep on an aircraft but my busy year caught up with me and I dozed off. My wife gave me a dig and told me to stop snoring. She protested that it was disturbing the other passengers.

We spent a week at the delightful Miss Maud's Swedish Hotel, taking day tours to Margaret River, Wave Rock, Pinnacles, wild flower areas and of course the WACA, the scene of many great cricket matches. Then it was time to head to the East Perth railway terminal for our trip across the Nullarbor Plain. Contrary to popular opinion. the arid 1100km plain is Latin not Aboriginal for 'no tree".

Long distance train travel was a new experience for me. I feared getting bored, so, although not an avid reader, I bought a book. My wife was more interested in looking at the countryside and the wild flowers alongside the track.

Twin cabins in Gold Service on the Indian Pacific have only limited luggage space and passengers have to restrict their carry-on luggage to immediate needs for the journey. After checking our excess baggage, we adjourned to the coffee shop to wait the boarding call.

As a copper for 30 years, I consider my powers of observation to be acute. When I am sitting around, I can't help myself. I like to study people. The coffee shop was busy, so while the missus was at the counter, I looked around at my fellow passengers.

My attention was attracted to a man, in his mid-50s, greying, well dressed denoting some affluence, with a very attractive blond woman holding his arm. The trophy wife, about half his age, was wearing significant expensive jewellery. With them were two young women – late teens, early twenties my guess not much younger than the trophy wife. There was a resemblance between these young women and the man indicating they were his daughters. Dad had obviously re-married. I wondered what the girls thought of step mum. She said something and when she looked away the girls sneered towards each other. All was not rosy there. I thought they would be business class air travellers rather than 'slumming' it on the train. I nicknamed them sarcastically the 'Happy Family.'

The next couple were elderly probably about 80 or so. They were both grey haired and fairly doddery. My guess was they were living their dream of traversing the Australian continent before their health or time ran out. Definitely adoring grandparents – maybe even great grandparents. I nicknamed them 'Gramps and Nan.'

Since 9/11 Muslims have been viewed with suspicion. Most Muslims I have met have been decent, law-abiding citizens. The Muslim couple were about mid-40s, nothing special. The woman was wearing the hijab head covering.

Many passengers were grey nomads, without their four-wheel-drives and caravans. I could imagine them in the outback, on the wallaby, hopping around from town to town. They were probably out spending the kids' inheritance. I tried to guess their former occupations. One tall man had a marching gait and could have been a soldier. Another with thick glasses gave me the impression of being an accountant. Some of the women I could see as school teachers.

A lone man attracted my attention. He had a dark complexion with thick black hair and well-trimmed beard. I thought mid-thirties, and, judging by his build, likely a gym junky. He could be either a bouncer or a heavy for some unpleasant organisation. I nicknamed him 'the Bouncer'.

With a toot from the train's whistle and a public address announcement, the coffee drinkers headed for their respective carriages. Coincidently, most of those I had been observing headed for our carriage. We were allocated carriage #9 with seat numbers 7 and 8. After boarding, the attendant came to inform us of our first meal time and how to book times for future meals. He also showed us how to operate the compact toilet and shower facilities in the cabin and the small safe for valuables.

I was amazed by the size of the Indian Pacific which has an average train length of 774 metres. Its décor oozes with the charm reminiscent of the great railway journeys in the world. The train does the 4352 km trip from Perth to Sydney in about 65 hours. One section of the line measuring 478km is the longest straight stretch of railway line in the world.

The train caters for Gold Service passengers in twin and single berth sleepers with meals and snacks provided in the Outback Explorer Lounge and the Queen Adelaide Restaurant Car. Red Service passengers have Day/Nighter seats with meals/snacks provided by the Matilda Café.

The train transports motor vehicles and I suspected that some of the grey nomads were railing their vehicles so as to experience train travel across the continent.

Gold Service fares include drinks in the Outback Explorer Lounge and Queen Adelaide Restaurant. I started to think that this trip was not a bad choice and a man could really enjoy partaking in the local beverages. The fares also included whistle-stop tours at Kalgoorlie, Adelaide and Broken Hill.

While the wife was watching the wild flowers and rolling countryside as the train sped along, I was quietly enjoying a drink and reading my book in the lounge waiting to be called for dinner. I was enjoying the book and found it hard to put down. The Happy Family entered through the automatic doors connecting the adjacent sleeping car with the lounge car. Something was being said and although I did not hear exactly what, the impression I gained was that not all was well. Dad went to the bar for drinks while the others sat down. Nothing was said between them and they seemed to be ignoring each other. This was going to be a very long trip for them.

Gramps and Nan entered both having movement difficulties exacerbated by their own unsteady gaits and the gentle rocking of the train. They sat down as soon as they could.

The Bouncer did not come so maybe he was in a later dinner sitting. Grey nomads appeared, chatting happily together.

Dinner was delightfully cooked by on-board chefs. The menu was not extensive but more than adequate in quality and quantity.

While most diners were enjoying their meals, war broke out in the Happy Family. Dad seemed to be trying to placate the trophy wife as the daughters appeared to be on the attack.

Gramps and Nan seated nearby looked most upset by the disturbance while most of the other diners and staff tried to ignore the situation. I had not noticed but the Bouncer had come in and was seated by himself. He was closely watching the dispute.

Our first whistle-stop tour was at Kalgoorlie. The train arrived at 10.30pm and the tour highlight was the visit to the rim of the very impressive Big Pit, a 3.6km wide open-cut gold mine. Below us we could see the massive trucks winding their way to and from the top of the pit. Another highlight was the street where the two remaining brothels in the town were located.

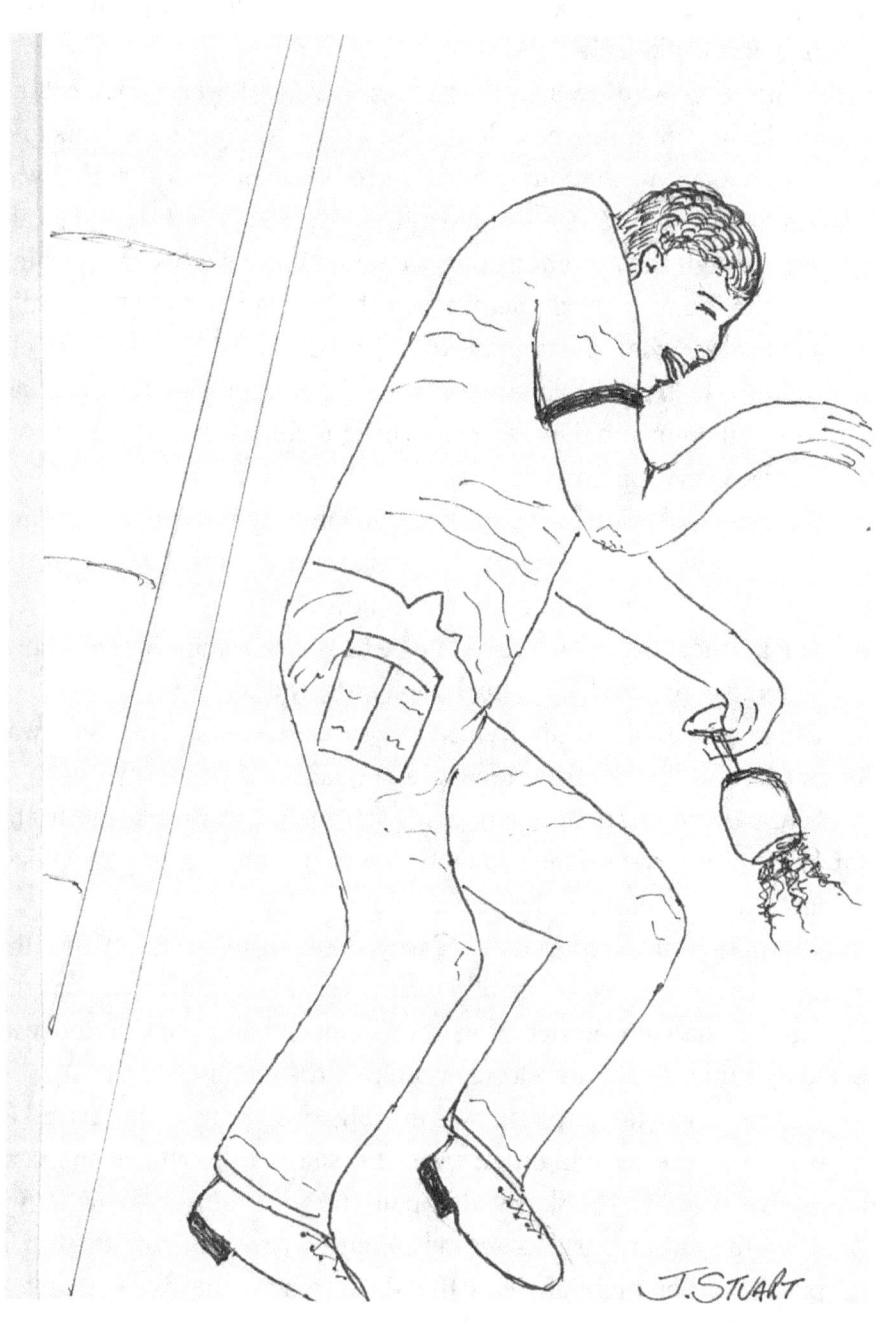

The next stop for refuelling was the settlement of Cook in South Australia. Cook once had a population of about 200 people but only a handful now remain. The settlement once boasted a school, hospital, golf course, swimming pool, tennis court, shops, jail and a hotel. These buildings and facilities are no longer used but remain a fascination for visiting tourists. The long dirt roads are used by aircraft and I watched a Cessna land and taxi up to the town manager's house. The pilot and a female passenger disembarked.

Back on the train, I settled into my book while the missus photographed the stony treeless plains of the Nullabor. It was that afternoon when it all happened.

The book was getting very interesting when I heard the loud scream from the next compartment. I quickly turned down the page corner so as not to lose my place and jumped up.

'He's dead!' the younger daughter of the man screamed. 'She's killed him. I knew she would.'

I pushed past the girl and entered the cabin. The man was slumped on the floor. There was no sign of a struggle. His lips were blue. I checked for a pulse but there was none. His laptop was on the floor. I am sure I would have heard something if there had been a disturbance but I did have my door shut.

The trophy wife accompanied by the tall man and his wife came down the carriage corridor.

'What's going on?' she screamed.

Before I could answer, the younger daughter yelled again, 'She killed him!'

'That's ridiculous,' she responded angrily. 'He has been having chest pains. It was probably a heart attack.'

While there was no blood or visual evidence of murder, hysteria was running rampant.

'Nobody go in there,' I stated firmly as I shut the door. 'This is a sudden death, which the coroner will have to investigate. Someone get the attendant.'

Heads were peering out the doors of the other cabins to find out what was going on. 'We have a problem but it is under control. Is anyone a doctor? We may need some assistance,' I asked just as the pale-faced young attendant came hurrying down the corridor.

It turned out that my 'accountant' was in fact a retired GP Can't get them right all the time. I explained that I was a Queensland Detective and I asked the GP to look at the body. At the same time my wife was trying to console the younger daughter who was joined by the older daughter. Both were hysterical. If looks could kill, step mum would have been dead from the glares given by the daughters.

After an examination of the body, the GP came out. He drew me aside.

'I was watching this fellow when the disagreement occurred over dinner and he looked healthy enough. Probably, some family stress involved. Without an autopsy, it is impossible to tell. I have seen a lot of heart attack victims and people who have overdosed both accidentally and intentionally but there is something wrong here. The way his face is contorted suggests that he may have been poisoned,' he reported.

I returned to the body, being careful not to tamper with any evidence. The man's arm was in an unusual position as if something had hit his neck and his hand was feeling for that area when he collapsed. A closer examination revealed a small puncture wound perhaps created by a syringe. I called the GP over. He confirmed my suspicion that a syringe could have delivered an unknown poison.

The thought crossed my mind: what would Poirot do in this situation? 'We will keep this to ourselves at this stage. Best not to upset the other travellers or alert the perpetrator to what we know.'

I carefully searched the cabin for any pills or poisons, photographing everything to preserve any evidence, but found nothing. I paid particular attention to the possessions of the trophy widow. She probably stood to gain most from the death but there was nothing to connect her to the suspected murder.

The sobbing trophy wife, now in the care of the tall man's wife, confirmed that her husband did have chest pains recently but he would not do anything about them. I told her that she would have to stay out of that cabin as the South Australian coroner would have to investigate. She was shocked but reluctantly agreed. The attendant found another cabin for her.

The daughters were not aware of their father's chest pains but apart from denigrating the step mum, they had no other useful suggestions to the cause of their father's death. They said he was a wealthy man with mining interests and that their mother had died from cancer a short time ago. Their father, much to their disgust, married the trophy wife whom they suspected of being after his money. She had mysteriously turned up after the mother's death and before they knew anything, she was moving in. The father had apparently hoped that the confines of the train journey might reduce the animosity the girls felt towards their step mother.

Police computers provide an enormous amount of information to assist in an investigation but this was not available, so it was back to the old days of good detective work.

The train's next stop was Adelaide, still some distance away, so I decided to conduct some preliminary inquiries. The train manager had been called by the attendant to notify the South Australian Police to meet the train on arrival.

I spoke to the doctor and his wife, a retired school teacher. They had seen nothing untoward. The wife had been dozing when the daughter's screams were heard.

The next cabin was occupied by the tall man, a retired soldier, and his wife who I found out was herbalist. They had been having a drink with the trophy wife in the Outback Lounge. They confirmed they had seen the man alive when the trophy wife joined them to go to the Lounge. The man was sitting with the cabin door open working on his lap top. They had knocked on the door of the cabin of the young girls to invite them to come but they had declined. Both were plugged into their iPads playing games. The thought crossed my mind that the herbalist could have concocted some poison to kill the man. This was interesting because the ex-soldier and the herbalist were providing the alibi for the trophy wife.

The Muslim couple were unhelpful, English not being their first language. I took the chance to glance around their cabin but there was nothing that would suggest their involvement.

Gramps answered the door of that cabin. Nan was asleep. He had heard nothing and seemed to be confused about what was going on.

The last cabin offered a surprise. It was occupied by the Bouncer – alone, so I thought. An attractive brunette woman opened the door. *Where did she come from?* I wondered. They also had nothing to offer but my curiosity was aroused by her appearance.

The attendant had not noticed anyone enter the carriage which necessitated passing his small end of carriage office.

If it was poison the murderer was probably a female as poison is usually considered a female murder choice. The trophy wife had an alibi and her husband was still alive when she left the cabin. The daughters were in their own cabin and had not seen their father for some hours. The younger daughter had gone to ask him something and found the door closed. She knew he should be there so she knocked. When he did not answer she opened the door and peered in. Her father was on the floor.

I pondered who may have had a motive. I presumed the trophy wife would benefit financially and that would be a strong motive. The daughters may want to circumvent any will changes by getting rid of dad first but the spouse would still have a claim. From the distressed reactions of the girls they did not appear likely murderers. The beneficiary or beneficiaries could have an accomplice to carry out the murder. I needed to find out if the man had any enemies. Perhaps a business associate or competitor might benefit financially from the death.

The other carriage occupants had no apparent motives although the woman with the Bouncer was intriguing. My brief conversation with them gave the impression that they were not recent acquaintances. The Bouncer may have been a contract killer but he would unlikely use poison. A professional killer would not have murdered on the train.

The daughters were still hysterical but I needed to find out more about the family. They told me their mum had been suffering from breast cancer but had seemed to be going into remission. Without warning she died and the death had been attributed to her condition. My ears pricked up when they told me how her face was contorted when she died in hospital. They did not know of any enemies their father had, although the mining downturn had placed strain on investors. He had a lot of Middle Eastern clients and I wondered whether the Muslim couple could have an interest.

The widow told me she had met her future husband after the death of his previous wife and she was able to console him. He was grateful to her for pulling him out of a depressive episode where he had contemplated suicide. She knew the girls did not like their father remarrying so soon after their mother's death but she had hoped to win them around in time.

When everyone including my wife went for dinner, I entered each cabin searching for clues. Normally I would get a warrant but there were no judges around here.

It wasn't until the last cabin that I found items which added to the mystery. Maybe there was an explanation. I needed to find out more.

Mobile phone reception was not available on this section of the track so I used the train's radio communications system to contact the Adelaide Homicide Branch. I needed inquiries carried out before the train arrived in Adelaide.

Any excitement over the trip had gone. The thought of the dead man lying in that cabin was enough to dampen anyone's spirits. For the rest of the journey to Adelaide I observed the suspects closely and read more of my book. Maybe I would find inspiration there.

I knew the South Australian detective who came on board in Adelaide. We had worked together on a number of cases before. I suggested we get the passengers in that carriage to meet in the Outback Lounge while the body was removed.

The inquiries I had requested proved very interesting indeed and confirmed my suspicions. Although this was not my jurisdiction, the SA Detective was happy for me to take the lead.

'Good morning everyone. Please take a seat,' I told the apprehensive group. After introducing my South Australian counterpart I went on, 'As you may be aware, I am a Queensland Homicide Detective. You have been asked here because there has been a sudden death and the coroner must undertake an investigation. As we were in the same carriage as the deceased, police will need statements for the coroner. I believe that the death was not a heart attack but was murder.'

There was gasp from the group and I watched for any reactions displaying guilt. Three people appeared uneasy at this revelation. The others appeared horrified.

I went on, 'I believe the deceased was sitting with the cabin door open when someone lunged in hitting him in the neck with a syringe containing poison. This would take an agile person with some knowledge of poisons. I am sure that an autopsy will discover the cause of death and identify the poison. I will go one step further to suggest that this is not the killer's first murder but the third.'

Again there was uneasy shuffling from three of the people present.

'Modern communications are a wonderful tool for investigators. While I did not have mobile reception the train has radio contact with stations on the line. I spoke to the SA police and they made some inquiries. Perth police were also very cooperative.'

By this time the three people started to look more uneasy. They knew the game was up but were trying to stay composed.

The widow was vehement. 'I had nothing to do with it. I loved my husband.'

'And your first husband as well,' I added. 'He was old enough to be your father too. Coincidentally, he had a heart attack. And the death of your second husband's wife was also suspicious. Her doctors thought she was recovering from her cancer when she died suddenly. Everyone thought her cancer was the cause and an autopsy was not performed. I believe they would have found that she had been poisoned. Fortunately she was buried and not cremated. Exhumation will tell us the truth about her death. There is only one person here capable of providing and delivering the poison.'

'It was their idea. I never wanted anything to do with it,' the trophy wife exclaimed pointing towards the other two uneasy passengers. Everyone turned to look at where she was pointing.

'That's absurd,' Gramps replied angrily. 'I could not have killed him and certainly my wife could not have done it. I am not well enough nor fit enough to do what was suggested.'

'That is funny, Gramps,' I said. 'Your real age is closer to 60 than 80 as is your wife's according to your drivers' licences. I must compliment you on your disguises. You had me fooled. A recently retired pharmacist who just happened to work at the hospital were the woman died would have knowledge of poisons and had the opportunity to kill her. Then you had the chance to introduce your suddenly widowed daughter to the woman's husband.'

'You will never prove that!' Gramps exclaimed.

'You should never have killed him on the train,' the trophy wife yelled. 'You said you would do it at Kalgoorlie at the mine pit and the body would never be found.'

'Shut up! You fool. We have done everything for you to set you up in life and this is how you repay us,' Gramps screamed back.

The gathered group were astounded and watched as the SA detective arrest Gramps, Nan and the trophy wife and escorted them from the train.

The South Australian detective had gathered information on the passengers. He found that the Bouncer was a Perth security provider employed by a large well-respected firm. The mystery brunette, his wife, was a solicitor delayed by a trial, causing her to miss the train. She had flown to Cook to catch up. The ex-soldier and his herbalist wife were apparently picked out to provide an alibi. The Muslim couple were from a Middle Eastern Embassy taking the opportunity to see Australia. The GP and ex-teacher were never suspects.

The death of the first wife concerned me. It had also troubled her doctors as she had apparently been going into remission. There had to be some connection to the death of her husband. The daughters had gone to the best schools in Perth and were currently at University. They appeared shaken by the death of their adored father so soon after the sudden loss of their mother.

Inquiries into the trophy wife produced some interesting facts. Perth police spoke to the deceased's business partners to identify competitors or associates who might have wanted want him dead. Nothing was revealed but all were critical of the trophy wife. She appeared after the death of the first wife and next thing the partners knew, he was marrying her. None expressed any liking for her and saw her as a distraction. The partners were genuinely concerned that she might have wanted want to take over running of the business through his estate. Police computer records did discover that she had been married before and that husband almost twice her age had died suddenly from a heart attack.

The most interesting information was about Gramps and Nan. My suspicions about them were raised when I looked through their cabin and found grey hair dye and clothing that would suggest the wearers were much younger. I found syringes in their cabin. While that may not be unusual given their age, it was cause for concern. The poison could have been disposed of after the death. Computer records found that, instead of pushing 80, they were only in their sixties. Further inquiries found that they had one child, a daughter, the trophy wife.

When I went back to our cabin my wife handed me my book.

'That was an interesting choice of books,' she said.

'Yes, it turned out to be rather prophetic – Agatha Christie's *Murder on the Orient Express*. Well Poirot solved the murder on the Orient Express. I solved the murder on the Indian Pacific.'

Prize-winning passionfruit at the Pine Rivers Show

THE TIME MACHINE

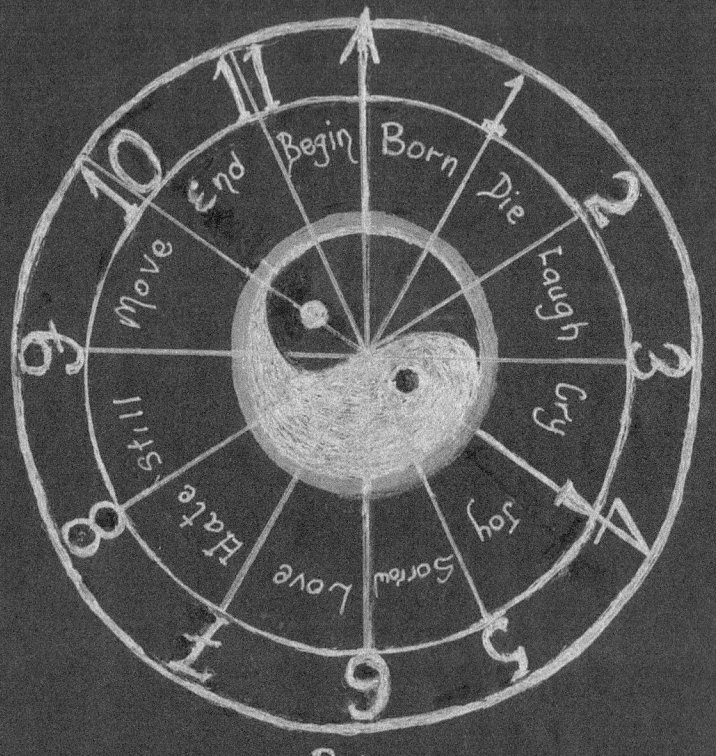

By
H G Wells

Illustrated by Margaret Brown

TIME WILL TELL
R. William Penshorn

I was Somewhere, Somewhere when I met a nice old man.
I felt he felt an interest in me, that's when it all began.
He said I looked familiar and asked if we'd met before.
I replied 'Not that I know of', and then he said some more

He told me I reminded him of himself some years ago.
Uneasiness crept over me. Why? I do not know.
He smiled at me and said 'Good luck', then left without delay
I knew within that he was me, many years away.

Next thing I knew I met a boy and strange though it may be
He looked quite familiar and reminded me of me.
I asked the boy how old he was. He said he'd just turned nine.
To my disbelief when I asked his name, it was the same as mine.

I scratched my head in wonderment and looked up to the sky
I looked back down at the little one and watched him wave goodbye
I woke up from a deep sleep and when I looked about
I saw my friend named Tim E Tock, it was him without a doubt

Tim was pleased to see me, he was an inventor.
He took me to his work shop, and there right in the centre,
Stood a peculiar contraption like I had never seen.
'What is it Tim?' I hastily asked. He answered 'A time machine.

'You my friend have just been travelling, to the future and the past.'
That's the moment everything fell right into place at last.
'You're a smart one Tim,' I said to him. 'You're on my clever list.
The only time machine I've ever known, is this watch upon my wrist.'

INSPIRED BY the H G Wells novel, *The Time Machine.*

SECOND CHANCE

Brenda Simcox-Hunt

KATHY had a busy day yesterday. She was pampered. She had a waxing, massage and facial. *A girl doesn't get married every day*, Kathy told herself. She didn't worry about the cost.

Her friends wanted her to go out with them last night but she told them she was going out to her parents' place. Her parents had phoned and asked her to go out to their place: but she told them she was going out with her friends. She wanted to be on her own.

Kathy awoke on Saturday morning, after a good night's sleep. She was too nervous to eat, so she made a banana and berry milkshake. Lazing around all morning, she tried to read but was too up-tight to concentrate. She filed and painted her nails. For lunch she had salad sandwich and a cup of coffee. The phone rang for the fourth time but again she ignored it. After lunch she had a long soak in the bath. Later she washed and set her long blonde hair in thick rollers. As a hairdresser, she knew how to do her hair to suit her large white hat.

Three o'clock came around and she began to do her make-up, trying not look into her eyes. Next she put on the corselet that pushed her small breasts up to flatter the neckline of her wedding gown. The white lacy stockings suited her long slender legs and her high-heeled shoes were enough to hold the dress off the floor.

She phoned for a cab, put on her hat and draped the short veil over her face. Picking up the little white purse that her grandmother had carried on her wedding day, she walked regally down stairs to the waiting taxi.

Betty Johnstone in the units over the road was feeling rather sad that day. She had finished her housework and went to the open window to shake out her duster. The sight she saw made her drop the duster out the window.

'No, no,' she shouted, as the taxi drove away from the curb.

She called to her husband who was on his computer in the spare bedroom. 'Jack, Jack, come quick.'

'What's wrong?' he said, as he came rushing into the lounge. He was shocked at the look of horror on his wife's face. 'Did you hurt yourself?'

'No, it's Kathy. She has just got into a taxi - in her wedding gown.'

'What? Wasn't Jonathon killed in Afghanistan six months ago?'

'Yes. Today would have been her wedding day. What shall we do?'

'What taxi did she take?'

'It was a Yellow Cab.'

'Hi. This is an emergency. One of your cabs has just picked up a fare from flat . . . .'

Jack looked over at his wife who mouthed the address. 'Unit four at 76 Highcrest Road, Lutwyche. Can you contact the driver?'

MARK Berry, a slim attractive man, didn't want to work that morning. His fourth year exam was due in five weeks. He couldn't believe he was almost at the end of his fourth year of studies. This time next year he would be doing his internship, and then the following year he would be Dr Mark Berry. That sounded so good. When Kieran phoned last night and asked him to do his shift, he couldn't refuse. Kieran had taken his shift eleven months ago when he had written himself off getting drunk when Beth had broken off their engagement. Mark liked taxi driving, he could choose his own hours and he loved driving around Brisbane. He knew where every suburb and entertainment centre was. Best of all, he could study during quiet times; he always took the relevant medical books with him in the cab. The call to Lutwyche was to be his last for the day. He was very surprised to see an elegant bride walk down from the flats and get in the back door.

'Hello,' he said in a friendly way, 'a big day today, is it?'

'Yes,' was the quiet reply.

'Where are your bridesmaids? Have they gone on ahead?'

'Something like that. Take me to the Story Bridge, please.'

'Okay.' Mark had a horrible feeling something was very wrong. The girl sounded and acted very strange. She should be happy and talkative. He looked in the rear-view mirror but he couldn't see her face through her veil.

'Are you having a quiet little wedding on the river bank?' he asked.

'Don't talk. Just drive,' she answered.

The trip only took ten minutes. Mark mentally sorted through his medical books to see how to handle this situation.

'Where do you want me to drop you? Down at the park under the bridge?'

She answered softly. 'Yes, thank you.'

Mark noticed she was not holding a bouquet. He drove slowly over the bridge and turned down the road leading to the park. There were lots of people picnicking but Mark could not see a wedding party anywhere.

'What time is the wedding? You seem to be early.'

'Just stop here, thank you. She handing over a bundle of notes.

'This should cover the fare.'

'Miss?' Mark was really concerned now. The girl got out of the taxi and began to walk towards the river.

_____ooo_____

MARGARET Smythe looked over at her husband Ted.

'Dear, let us go over to Kathy's flat. I have an awful feeling.'

'You know she said she was going to Michelle's house.'

'Yes. I know but something is wrong. I am feeling panicky. Let's go right away. You back the car out while I get my bag.'

When they arrived at the flat they saw Betty and Jack from over the road, talking to a police officer outside Kathy's block of flats. Margaret jumped out of the car as soon as Ted pulled up.

'What's wrong Betty?' She called as she ran over.

'Oh, Margaret. I'm so glad you are here. Kathy went off in a Yellow Cab about ten minutes ago. She was wearing her wedding dress.'

'Oh Ted,' Margaret said, grabbing his hand. 'I told you I had an awful feeling'

'What's happening, Officer?' Ted asked 'Betty has probably told you our daughter was to be married today. But her fiancé was killed in Afghanistan six months ago. Have you been able to get on to the taxi company?'

'Yes, Sir. Mr Brown here was able to contact the company. The driver is not answering his radio though. A squad car is on its way to the Story Bridge, which is the destination the driver gave the office.'

____ooo____

MARK parked the taxi and watched the bride walk down towards the river. He realized what she was going to do. He jumping from the car and ran after her. He caught up with her as she was about two metres away from the river. He had noticed other people were hurrying towards her too.

'Don't do this.' He grabbed her around the waist.

'Leave me alone,' she sobbed. 'I've got nothing to live for now Jonathon's dead.' She struggled to get out of Mark's arms. Her hat fell off in the struggle. Tears welled in Mark's eyes as he saw the sorrow in her eyes. He held her tighter instead.

'I know how you feel. My fiancée broke off our engagement eleven months ago.' 'But she's not dead. Jonathon won't ever be coming home.'

'You can get through this. I did, and you can too.'

'Excuse me.' An authoritative voice spoke. 'Is she the passenger you picked up at Lutwyche?'

'Yes,' Mark answered, trying to wipe the tears from his eyes as he held the sobbing girl to his chest.

'We will look after her, Sir,' the police officer said. 'You can let her go now.'

'Where will you take her?' Mark's voice trembled with emotion.' I am a medical student. I believe this young lady is in deep shock.'

'We will take her to the Royal Brisbane Hospital. She will be looked after there. Her parents are on the way there too.'

'What is your name?' Mark asked the now quiet girl.

'It's Kathy Smythe. I'm alright now. Thank you for stopping me. What's your name?'

'Mark Berry.'

'Mark, will you come to the hospital and see me, please?'

'Yes, I will. I will be there in a little while.'

Mark watched as Kathy, as regal as a princess, walked away with the police officers. He knew he had to help her. He suddenly felt as if his life was a whole lot brighter.

INSPIRED BY hope.

QUEENSLANDER
Bakthi Ross

A tall roof,
Wooden verandah,
Sitting on a rocking chair,
Watching the birds.

Summer heat,
Homemade lemonade,
A sip of cool breeze,
A calming gas in a hot fire.

Heat waves,
Mirages of expectations,
Nothing will change the summer heat,
We wear it and we sweat it.

Queenslander,
Tanned and tough,
Dusty boots and checkered shirts,
Akubra off the head,
To cover the face from the heat.

A midday sleep,
An unwanted wait,
The nature's rest,
Leaves craving in thirst,

A moving sun,
A following shadow,
Brings back the evening breeze,
Queenslander off again,
To work until dusk.

Queenslander is the name,
That moves with the season,
You cannot bend or break,
Without the sun's order.

He sleeps until dawn,
And moves with the sun,
A Queenslander!
An inspiration.

" SUMMER "   Inspired by Vivaldi " Four seasons "

Cicadas singing theirs summer melody,
The steady plundering sound of the sea,
In the heat of summer's midday sun….
The world is at peace.
It last only an instant and then it cease…
Take that minute, hold it long,
Make that minute to last that song,
The song of "That summer" in your life,
Where the harvest was so ripe.
The memory then will last,
Very well after the summer's past…
And the autumn of your life will be…
Delighted with the most precious memories.

Lillian E. Ves-Tebesceff (L.Ves-Te)

THEATRE

SHERWOOD

R. William Penshorn

HI, my name is Ramon Sherwood. I have stumbled through life tackling whatever came my way. Some call me a soldier of fortune. Recently I have been involved with a property-development venture.

A while ago I walked a city street and saw a man outside a movie theatre carrying sandwich boards which advertised the current feature. It read, 'Now Showing *A Tale of Two Cities*.' The man was not exactly as bright as a button. He stood there and cried out, 'Come and see it ladies and gentlemen, *A Sale of Two Titties*.' The passers-by were amused by his mix up of words and took it in their stride.

I knew the theatre manager, a nice guy named Ken Perry. It so happened he was there and I said, 'G'day'. We joked about his advertising man and he told me he would have to get rid of him in the coming week when the next program was due to start.

'Why's that?' I asked. 'Everyone seems to take him light heartedly and in good spirit.'

'Our next feature film is 'Friar Tuck,' Ken explained.

'Oh,' I said. 'Say no more.'

Before I continued on my way I took note of the admission prices and remembered in my younger days when everything cost so much less. We would go to the 'flicks' as they were called, see two films, cartoons, newsreels and trailers of coming events.

Often an episode of a serial would be included. *Sir Galahad*, and *Batman and Robin* were a couple of favourites. [The Batmobile was a '49 Chevrolet back then.)

Everyone would stand for the National Anthem at the start of the show. At interval handsome young men and pretty teenaged girls would walk the aisles with trays strapped around their necks selling peanuts, popcorn, Crackerjacks and jelly apples. Round, dark orange sweets

81

called Jaffas were a firm favourite. The 'in thing' was to roll them down the aisle as far as possible.

One thing in favour of today's visit to the theatre is the lack of the smell of smoke. Cigarettes, pipes and cigars have been banned. Candy fags are still permitted. I remember in my childhood school days, a young smart Alec smoking away with his mates not realizing his parents were sitting right behind. His mother tapped him on his shoulder. He responded by twisting his head slightly and exhaling smoke all over her face. He came to regret that action very quickly.

As I continued on my way, I thought to myself about how the prices of everything kept on going up, skyrocketing. I had put myself into considerable debt to acquire an eighty-acre property which I planned to develop into real estate allotments.

I had soon got to know why some of the local council members were referred to as 'Little Hitlers'. One of them in particular was giving me hell. He was a pale, weedy, freckle-faced man named Ross Whitfield.

When I first approached the council, he agreed to inspect the property with me. 'Y' know,' he had said, 'There's a lot of profit to be made here on this venture. We're prepared to cooperate with you if you're prepared to cooperate with us.' He gave me a sickly wink and proceeded to pat his open hand which was undoubtedly a gesture to 'grease his palm'.

'Get my drift?' he said.

You little worm, I thought.

I got his drift all right and it annoyed me to the hilt but I did not let on. I decided to play his game until the time was right. At a follow-up meeting not too much later, Ross had put it to me to slip him fifty thousand dollars on the quiet. For that he would ensure everything ran smoothly.

'If you don't play along,' he threatened, 'I'll create hell for you and you'll come out a lot worse off in the long run.'

I saw red but controlled my emotions and pretended to, as he put it, 'play along'.

I found out Ross was married to Beth, a decent woman, the daughter of a wealthy business man named Jeff Gardiner and his wife, Robyn.

The Gardiners resided in a waterfront mansion. It fronted a surf beach and backed onto a canal where Jeff moored his luxury launch. The Gardiners were a God-fearing couple who lived life on the straight and narrow. They were not overly fond of Ross but, unlike the rest of Beth's few beaus, he had asked for her hand in marriage. Jeff and Robyn had hopes and dreams of becoming grandparents someday and accepted Ross for what he was.

Ross took comfort in having Beth as his wife, knowing she was heiress to a small fortune that someday he would share. He had a roving eye but he took extreme measures to prevent Beth knowing of this.

He found he had most luck with the fairer sex when he was prepared to part with a fistful of dollars.

I had been keeping in touch with Mandy Korn, a girl I had known since college days. She was a nice kid but fate had treated her somewhat unkindly. In recent times she had become a 'party girl' making a little cash on the side from being a shade more than friendly with certain gents.

Sometime earlier, Mandy had crossed paths with a suave handsome man named Blair Dellar. They shared a whirlwind romance. Blair was a successful business man. He made his fortune as an importer. He mainly dealt in jewellery: rings, necklaces, bracelets, wrist watches and the like. Rumour had it he was involved in drug trafficking. If it were true, he was clever enough not to get caught. Further rumour had it the police were in on it. Who knows? Mandy was totally in love. She envisaged she would marry Blair someday and spend the rest of her life with him.

Her dreams all came to an abrupt end one evening when she and Blair were dining at a high class restaurant. A well-dressed glamorous blonde appeared. She was clad in a low-cut red dress, hemmed just below the knee. It had a generous slit in one side revealing her shapely leg. She wore matching red high-heeled shoes and a diamond studded necklace. She sat without invitation at their table to join them. 'Hello Blair,' she said. 'Who's this?' Blair reddened and forced himself to say, 'Er Mandy, I'd like you to meet Shirley, my wife.' Mandy stood, glared at Blair in disbelief. 'You never told me you were married, you, you cad.' She picked up her hand bag and walked off. That was the end of that.

I gave Mandy a call and arranged to meet her. I told her about 'Ross the Rat' as I now thought of him. She agreed to help me out. We set up some hidden cameras in her apartment bedroom. I explained I was to meet Ross at the Fox Hotel Beer Garden for further discussions.

The plan was for Mandy to meet me, supposedly by chance, and show mock interest in Ross and lure him away. He took the bait like a hungry snapper. Ross called Beth and lied to her that he would be home late as he was required to be at a meeting. His story was more a twist of the truth than a lie. He was going to be home late and he was going to be at a meeting but not exactly the kind of meeting Beth envisaged.

When Ross arrived at Mandy's apartment, he had no earthly idea he was about to appear in a movie, let alone in the starring role. When it was time to go, he departed with a smug expression of satisfaction. 'I dare say we should get it together more often,' he said to Mandy. Mandy shrugged. 'You had a good time then?' She said it with a forced smile.

'Sure did,' Ross croaked with a creepy grin. He got into his Mercedes and sang along with his stereo CD player all the way home. One of the tracks was Hank William's *Your Cheatin' Heart*

A day later Mandy unashamedly showed me several photos of the unsuspecting lustful Ross. I wasted no time in meeting up with him to announce I was not going to go along with his selfish criminal demands.

He glared at me in disbelief. 'You'll pay dearly for this,' he grunted.

'Maybe you'll think differently when you check out these recent snaps,' I said. 'And you'll be interested to know, there also is a movie.'

Ross gritted his teeth, wanting to scream abuse. He could find no words.

'By the way, the negatives are all in a safe place, and I don't really have to arrange for Beth and her parents to view them.' I remember well not being able to hold back a grin.

Normally pale Ross the Rat, turned the colour of a beetroot and began to shake. He wiped the sweat from his brow. 'You bastard,' he snarled half under his breath. 'That's blackmail.'

I looked him straight in the eye. 'So it is,' I agreed. 'I thought you'd recognize that.'

'Okay, okay! Go ahead and do as you wish. I know when I'm screwed.'

'Don't worry, I will,' I said. 'And it seems to me this would not be the first time you have been guilty of pulling this kind of foul deed, Ross'

'So what? You can't prove anything.'

'Maybe not but from what I have observed, your nest seems to have quite a few more feathers than that of the average councillor. You and your new Mercedes, your wife with the latest BMW etcetera, etcetera!'

'What are you getting at? Damn you,' he cursed.

'Listen up. That fifty grand of mine you tried to swindle is staying in my pocket. Three of my favourite charities are the Red Cross, the Salvation Army and the Surf Life Savers.'

'What's that got to do with it?' he growled.

'I want you to pay fifty grand to each of the three out of your own pocket. Do you hear me?'

'That's plain daylight robbery,' he protested.

'You'll pay it though, won't you?'

'Yes, yes, I'll bloody well do it. You win.'

'Good.'

'When do I get the photos?'

'You'll get the photos, the negatives and everything as soon as my development is complete and signed over, no strings attached.'

I have never seen such a look of despair as I did on the face of Ross the Rat at that moment.

'Alright! Alright! Have it your way,' he muttered, then stood up and walked away.

I caught up again with Mandy later that day. We had a few drinks and shared a few laughs. In due course my project was completed and I am pleased to say, without a hitch.

Ross kept to his word and so too did I. When the maintenance period for the parklands was up and it was time for the council to take over, I handed the negatives and photos to Ross, both stills and movies, all except one, but he does not know that.

As for now, well I made a small bundle out of my real estate venture, put aside as much as I needed to get by for a while and spread the rest among what I consider to be society's most needy causes.

Right now, I'm just breezing along with the breeze, wondering what exciting adventure lies in store.

I just noticed as glamorous blonde walk by. She turned her head to give me the 'once over'. I just caught the hint of a smile. Things are looking good.

THIS STORY was inspired by the many legends of Robin Hood. He robbed the unworthy rich and helped out the needy.

" AUTUMN " Inspired by Vivaldi " Four seasons ".

The wind is blowing
The leaves are falling
At my feet.
The sky is low
The clouds are grey
Autumn is in!
Short days are coming
We all be going
Down with the flu.
Hot lemon toddy
In large mugs
Will satisfy....
The dream...
Blue sky, green trees,
-Eternal Spring-.
Who are you fooling?
The leaves are not falling
The trees are green,
You are in Queensland,
No need to dream,
You've got –Eternal Spring-

Lillian E. Tebesceff (L.Ves-Te)

THE CUBE
Kerry Hall

Dear Honoured Customer,
The cube yours to open, stand back to prepare.
Follow the script, be precise; be very aware.

It is more than before, one player is all.
To command your large army of Morphids and Tors.
Just think of your move, the creatures will know.
They are fierce battle ready, and blood lust will show.

It is time to play now, the Game Master's hand.
Just yours against mine, this battle be grand.
Good luck to you all, who will challenge me thus.
Take a bow, battle hard, and enjoy this I trust.

The time limits set, two hours no more.
Then return to the Master, the next to explore.
Place your order, be quick, take a chance, heed the call.
Own the one of its kind, the best game of them all.

INSPIRED BY- H.G Wells' *The Island of Doctor Moreau.*

THIS BREATH

Kate Tomsett

GAZING across the war-torn desert of Iraq, Ashish jumped from the tank to return to the US base. Whack! The intoxicating cloth swallowed Ashish's head and the gun barrel, cold as death, stabbed his back. That lifeless beat of ISIL's war drum is silent and deadly.

That was the last moment of the outside world Ashish remembered before he woke up in the ISIL base, surrounded by the bloody silver bars of his cage. He knew the US would never condone ransom; he had worked for them long enough. That wasn't news to ISIL, either. That's why Ashish was tortured for information, unlike his fellow captive Christians and reporters.

'What is the plan for US? What are they building? What do you know?' The masked devil screamed such questions before Ashish's skin turned purple. Back home, Ashish worked for the US government as their leading ammunition and security specialist. There, his wife and two girls were left to believe in the disguise created by the distance. At least they could still believe that Daddy was safe at the US base and would be home for Christmas. Ashish fought for his life but also to return home.

For the first weeks of Ashish's capture his only focus was escape. After an endless session of questioning, whipping and beating, Ashish limped towards his cell and the blood from his back trailed behind him. Although uncertain of the time, Ashish knew it had to be the early hours of the morning, as the limited guards were slumped and heavy eyed. Pulling the deep wounds of his back apart, Ashish summoned all his strength to lash the chains that bound his hands across the temple of his escort. Before the guard fell to the floor, Ashish sprinted through his searing pain and followed his blood trail. Blazing through the maze of bullets, he heard the gunfire of the guards bounce off the walls and whistle across the hairs of his head. Ashish attempted to find refuge around the sharp corner and his frantic search detected a concealed door.

The thud of his heartbeat bashed Ashish's ears as the harrowing darkness amplified his fear. The walls burst with air. Gas. Ashish held his breath, anxiously anticipating the hell of his next inhalation. Beating against the door his skin was exposed to a different degree of burn: chemical. The blistering acid sent every inch of Ashish's body into shock and he fell unconscious.

In the terror of his daze Ashish woke through screams. He survived, but his capture rose to another intensity. No longer did bars surround him but cold steel walls: no windows, only darkness. Ashish learned escape was impossible so from that moment forward he focused on making the most of the little life he had left. Ashish knew he could cause greater damage from inside the complex than behind their enemy's firing line.

Every dawn, although impossible to witness in constant darkness, marked the beginning of what could be Ashish's last day. He had worked to make the most of everything in his destroyed life, never knowing what second might be his last. Life is a right, not collateral or casual. Every beat played on Ashish's skin drove his passion for peace, as he was disgusted to be the skin of their war drum. Every word whispered, questioned or encoded, Ashish would spend his days piecing together. He prayed for the day he might find a piece of the puzzle to stop this senseless war.

The cage slammed open. Ashish was abused, blindfolded, restrained and taken to his torture chamber.

'What tracking does the US have on us?' the balaclava demanded. Ashish remained silent and resisted any thoughts of the painful consequence.

'What is the security code to break their firewall?' Ashish persisted in mental strength and belief that he would die but ISIL would never benefit from his capture. The hot breath of his persecutor was all the blinded Ashish sensed before a blade was launched deep into his side. Scarlet trickled from Ashish but he refused to give them any satisfaction.

'Hurry the hell up, al-Barghdadi has given us ...' the earpiece hidden in the balaclava inconspicuously muffled. Ashish had grown reliant on his hearing with the amount of time he spent blindfolded. But never had he heard anything this significant. The last piece of information was agonisingly encoded. The real torture for Ashish: not knowing the code. This would be his key to craft his own war drum, one with the rhythm of peace.

Ashish was thrown back into his cell, left to sit in his pooling blood. Desperate to hear another call through the earpiece he taunted the persecutor.

'I have what you need!' Ashish cried through his split and swollen mouth. Immediately the guard raced back to drive his boot into the open wound. Ashish's façade was shattered as he fell to the floor in excruciating pain. Yet, the punishment was too short lived for any more interception. Ashish was compromised and his window of opportunity was slamming shut.

'I know... I know the codes.' The words staggered out of his mouth leaving their bitter and poisonous taste. Finally, the persecutor was forced to consult the earpiece. Ashish strained to hear anything, as he was jolted to his feet; nothing.

As Ashish was escorted through the darkness he couldn't help but be disgusted in himself. About to give up information which could kill thousands of people while he plays with the chance to understand some stupid code. 'I cannot be played. Their war drum will remain silent and my skin will never provide a beat or rhythm to their roar of terror,' pounded his determined subconscious.

Bright lights broke Ashish's trance as he was tied down to the cold, metal bench. What would he tell them? The truth, and risk the catalyst of World War three- or a lie and die being an expendable.

'What is the code?' the broken English asked complacently. The decisions raced through Ashish's head only creating more confusion.

'I will only share them with your leader.' Ashish awaited the blow of pain, as he knew his arrogance would not go unpunished. But the minion needed direction from his master. 'ال عام ال دعآل م للا ازدهر' the repeated encoded message echoed through Ashish's mind as he was knocked unconscious. Without negotiation Ashish's limp body was dragged through the compound to reach the control centre. He was surprised it happened so quickly; they must be desperate.

Restrained to a new chair Ashish groggily pulled open his heavy eyelids to see that computers and surveillance equipment surrounded him. The icy steel of the gun barrel was forced against his temple. Whether these codes did or didn't work, Ashish knew his fate. Before him was the US firewall with information on ISIL. No way in hell would they let Ashish live after he witnessed this. Only his wrists were released from the chair. Ashish's pale hands fearfully rattled over the keys. The adrenaline shot through his body as he ploughed through the initial security walls desperately hoping the US system would not fight back. He needed to find these codes. Flash, the screen blinked with the encoded ISIL information. That brief second launched Ashish out of his agony but into a new state of panic. The date was the first thing that struck Ashish. The 31st of December, 11:45 pm. He had been stranded in this hellhole for eight months. More than life, Ashish focused to keep the image of the code captured in his mind. Desperately attempting to fit the pieces of this puzzle, Ashish managed to translate, 'ال دعآل م للا زدهر ال عام' to 'raey mohoalbla noitarepo'. But, even in English, it made no sense. He worked so hard to see meaning behind this key to save his life. The time spent distracted forced the gun deeper into his skull. There was no time. Ashish had to get through the firewall to buy himself some time, but he couldn't help spend it straining his broken mind for answers. There, in the message 'Allah' was hidden. Ashish removed their decoy and spelt the message backwards, 'Operation Boom Year'.

Ashish just wanted the gun to fire; that message meant nothing. Nothing! His fatigued mind collapsed as he broke into shattering tears.

Ashish's time had run out. He was forced in front of a camera. The executioner's blade was sharpened and resting on his neck; his head forced back for slaughter.

'Any last words?' the executioner's dark voice sent Ashish's mind into a spiral.

'You will never win. Evil will never conquer. The ball is a bomb!' Ashish screamed as his head fell away from his shoulders.

A million live-streamed New York viewers raced for their lives out of Times Square. It was 11:59 pm in New York at the highly celebrated New Year's Eve Ball Drop. A million lives were saved because Ashish cracked the code. If that ball dropped the mass-murdering explosion would've marked the New Year. One life sacrificed for a million. Peace made in a time of war.

INSPIRED BY Suheir Hammad, *What I Will*

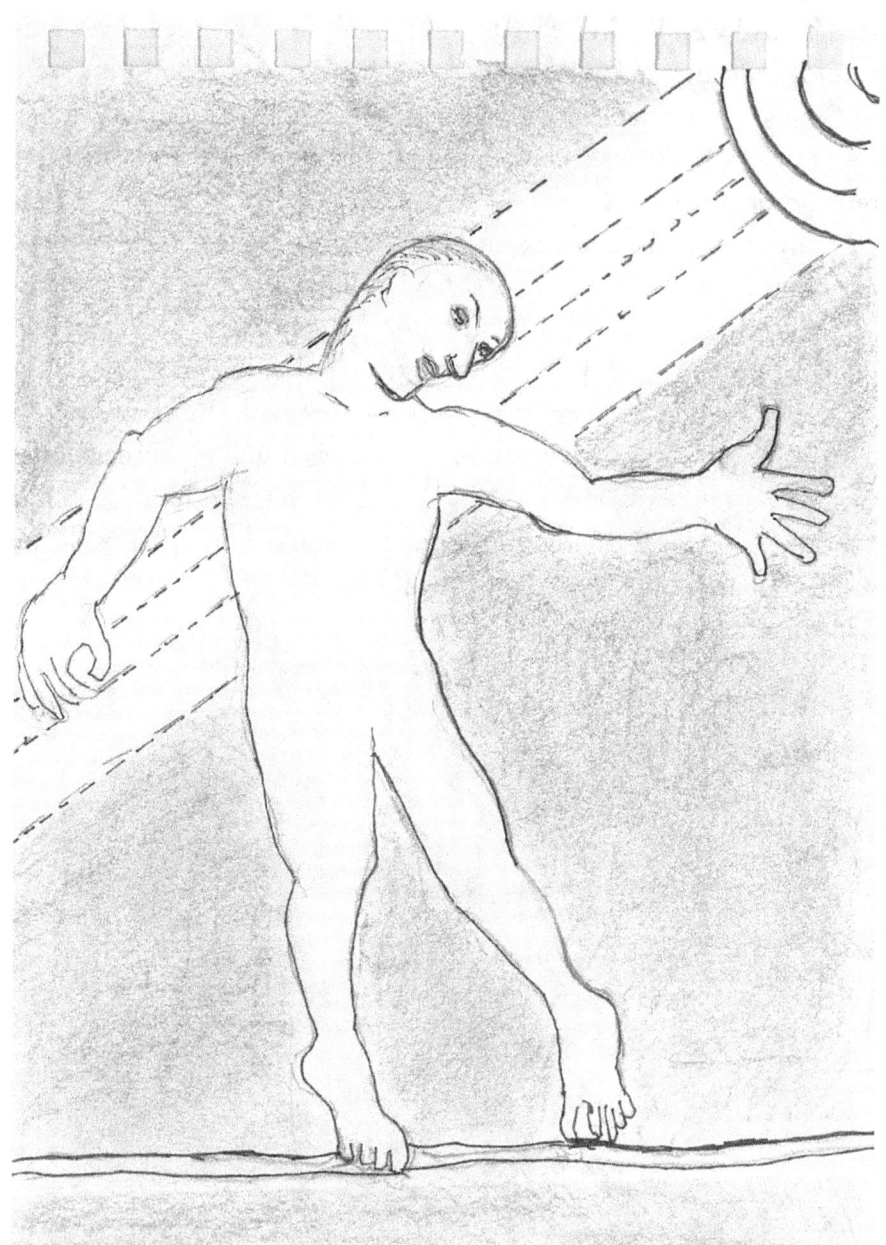

SEE YOURSELF IN A FRAMED PICTURE

Bakthi Ross

Mourn for that loss,
Yearn for that happiness once you had had.
Loss is such a painful emotion,
It drains you of your desires of life.

You cry.
You sit in silence,
You watch those pictures and enjoy those
Past moments.
Then the tears run out of you
Like the rolling pearls of emotions.

That picture you carry in you
And in your mind carries you over those
Hurdles of Life.

Loss is a picture of an emotion,
You picture yourself in a framed painting.
You colour your background,
You let that light shine through the darkness,
You draw over the ups and downs of the landscape.
You let that water flow over those difficult rocks.
When you finished that picture,
It reflects all the emotions of that framed loss.

Once you are out of that framed picture,
You can see the clear picture of yourself.
Now you can move on to the next picture
Of your life.

Lillian Tebesceff

THE LONG ROAD BACK

Mikael Koch

'. . . ARE you listening to me?'

I snap out of my daze, slowly returning to reality. I have been doing that a lot lately; letting my mind wander to pastures greener than the dark place where it usually resides. I know I should be paying attention during all of these sessions – they have been set up purely to try and help me 'assimilate back into society'. But when the entire reason you have to come to these blasted things is to try and fix what you tried so hard to hide away inside yourself, it is easy to pretend no one is there. Instead, I am faced with the young, innocent face of someone who has never seen the brutalities of war; never had their friends fall around them; never seen the light slowly drain . . .

'I understand how hard this must be for you, but in order to get past this; you need to work with me.'

I look up at him with bloodshot eyes, and can immediately see him start to fidget under my gaze. How can he possibly understand how hard it was for me to survive, to escape with my life from a place where lives are being taken all around me.

'Gas! GAS! Quick, boys!'

No! Just as I was starting to put that blasted time behind me. I do not want to start remembering again; not now, not ever. God knows I have suffered enough already; had to live with the fact that I left so many good men behind on those fields of hell. I can already see the look of pity start to form on his face, as they always do when I have these flashbacks. They have been happening ever since I came back from The Great War; making sure I could enjoy its 'greatness' for the rest of my life.

When they first started happening I thought it would only be a matter of time before they faded, before I was able to move on. I thought I would be able to escape from them by drinking my sorrows away. It was only after two years of torment that I finally realised that I would not be able to escape from those times, would never be able to forget everything, that I couldn't stop no matter how hard I tried.

He looked at me with a stupid grin on his face, knowing full well that he'd won once again.

'Looks like another lot of tobacco for me. You really need to stop betting all of your precious possessions away, it's not like you get many of them around here.'

'This time I'll win and get all of it back Tom, and then you won't be smiling for long!'

'That's what you said the last four times, and look where that's gotten you.'

'ALRIGHT YOU LOT – STOP YOUR DILLY DALLYING! IT'S YOUR TURN BACK IN THE TRENCHES.'

I think about the few positive moments always cut short. But at least they were there. It made us come together as a sort of family, albeit a dysfunctional one. Without the support of my brothers in arms, I would not have been able to get into the trench – let alone get out of it in one piece. But for all the help they gave me, I could not save the one person who did the most for me.

As the shell hit nearby we both lay down to avoid as much of the shrapnel as possible. We hadn't even noticed they'd started approaching us until they were right next to the trenches. In just those few short moments when the shots started firing we'd probably lost about half our company; and the other half didn't seem like they'd hold on for much longer. I saw Tom on the other side of the trench, using his rifle to take down as many of the enemy as he could.

In the safety of his friends he was the nicest man you could ever meet; but when you put him in a situation where those same friends were in danger – he was like the devil incarnate. He would go into battles against unbelievable odds and escape with barely a scratch to show for it.

I tried to run towards him; tried to help him get out of there once more; tried to get him back to where he could save lives instead of taking them. He bayonetted a German soldier as he charged him, and when he saw me coming to try and help him – gave me a smile to let me know it would all be okay; that we'd make it back together.

That was when he was shot.

'. . . Are you okay? Do you need a moment, a drink of water?'

Just thinking about that moment; that singular point in time where I knew my best friend in the entire world was gone – it brought me to tears. I knew that I was starting to well up, and that the counselor would want me to discuss 'how I felt' – as if that would make the memories go away. It was because of my stupidity; my need for support when everyone else was able to survive by their own two legs, that took him away. 'I...I need some space. Can we just stop for this week?'

Before he could even respond I rushed out of the room and onto the street. How can I even live with myself if I know that I caused one of the most kind and caring people in the world to die in a foreign land? I could not even do anything about it; could not find the people who had done it to him and made them suffer for robbing the world of such a life.

I could not even let his family know myself, for I was deemed to be too 'mentally insecure' to head home immediately. They sent me to so many therapists and psychiatrists I lost count, in order to try and make me the model soldier that they showed to the world – brave, strong and proud – when in reality I was anything but.

After a while they simply gave up on me, sent me home as a broken man with a broken life.

I walked to the side of the road and looked down at the rocks below. Maybe it would be better if I just ended my life before I caused anyone else harm. I cannot integrate into society. I cannot make the world a better place. I cannot even keep my own life together. As I started to climb over the barrier between me and Tom, I remembered.

'Look, I know how much you're struggling. You think you may as well sacrifice yourself for the country since you have no chance of surviving anyway? Well we're both getting out of here alive. I'm telling you that right now. These bloody Germans aren't going to get the best of us, are they? We're surrounded on all sides with no help in sight! We may as well go out and take down as many of them as we can, instead of cowering inside these trenches, waiting to die' Don't throw away your life so lightly – You have people back home who need you! You can't just run out into a meat grinder just because you think we have no chance to escape. We MUST escape. For the sakes of our friends and family we WILL get out of this mess, and we WILL go home and put their fears to rest.

'We are not dying today.'

...and stopped. If I die today, I throw away the sacrifice Tom made to get me home. While he didn't make it back, I owe it to him to make a difference to the world; show everyone how it is not 'sweet and right to die for your country'. If I do not do that, I will not be able to look him in the eye when I make it to the other side. It is my duty. So this time when I walk into the counselling room, I do so with the thoughts of Tom inside me, helping me to succeed.

INSPIRED BY *Dulce and Decorum Est* by Wilfred Owen.

PAPPY

Caitlyn Heathwood

EVEN sleeping his breathing was staggered. Once more her senses were overpowered by the sanitisers and disinfectants. She sat motionless and watched the rise and fall of his chest. *It's okay*, she kept telling herself. *He's still here, he's still alive.* It was hard to believe that this man lying before her was the same man she had known her whole life.

She sat back in her chair suddenly exhausted by the thought of undergoing this man's daily assault of pills, tests and needles. With the abrupt movement, the chair shifted along the floor, moaning in protest. The noise rattled her body, already tense from the weight her mind was carrying.

'What's with all the racket, Kiddo?'

Clara turned to see his kind eyes smiling over at her, traces of sleep clinging to his face.

'Sorry Pappy, I didn't mean to wake you.' She knew that he needed all the rest he could get in the state he was in.

For a moment neither spoke. They sat in each other's company, comfortable enough to withstand the fierce grip of absolute silence.

'Well, don't just sit there like a frightened mouse, I don't bite, ya' know.' He extended his arms as high and wide as he was able to.

As she embraced his frail body she realised just how much the cancer had taken from him. She could feel each of his brittle ribs through his gown. She squeezed as hard as she dared.

From before she could remember, this man had been a beacon of hope and generosity, her definition of strength. Now, as she held him in her arms she felt his life slowly seeping through her embrace. The fear that filled her body caused her to impulsively grip him tighter, for she felt if she let go she risked losing him forever. He shifted in her arms.

She realised what she had done and, despite her desire to remain in his embrace, quickly pulled away, now sitting on the edge of his bed. 'I'm so sorry, I didn't mean to. I don't know what's gotten into me. Are you okay? If you're not, I can get a nurse to bring in some pain killers. Actually I'll just go get a nurse. Yes, that's . . . '

'Whoa, whoa, whoa! Calm down Kiddo. It's okay, I'm alright, just a bit tender. Ya' know the story.'

She nodded. However at that moment, while she knew the full story, she knew that for him there were a few missing pieces. The doctor's words ran through her mind. *Legally we have to tell you, there is one last procedure . . . it may give you hope.*

With her mind running wild, she was unable find her voice. Instead she just looked at him hoping that he understood the extent of her remorse for his earlier discomfort.

He obviously read deeper into her mind than she anticipated, 'Hey, I've known you long enough to know when something's troubling ya, kid. Is there something you're not tellin' me?'

'Well, yeah . . . There's, um.' She tried to find the words.

She knew that this was his last hope. The doctors thought that he might not be strong enough. However, unlike the doctors, who knew him through a collection of numbers and readings, she knew his true character; he was a fighter. She had to tell him in a way that made him understand the severity of the situation. She refused to let him die without exhausting every possible treatment or trial. 'I need you to listen to what I'm about to say, and I mean really listen to me. Can you do that?'

'Of course I can. I'm all ears.' He watched her with such intent she found it hard to hold his gaze.

'I know you have been through so much. I know that with each day that passes you find it just that little bit harder to do things that you used to take for granted.' She paused expecting him to interject saying that he was fine and that she should worry less. He didn't. It troubled her, but she continued. 'I'm just going to cut to the chase. I was talking with the doctors earlier today and they say that there is one last thing that we can try. There is this new radical treatment where they . . . well, I'll get them to explain it to you later, they will do a better job than I would be able to.'

Once again she waited for him to speak. Instead he just looked past her as if engaged in an internal argument.

'Don't you see Pappy? There is still a chance, there is still hope.'

He no longer looked through her. 'You're right. There is still hope but it doesn't lie in an experimental treatment.'

Clara was confused, *what was he talking about?* This was their only remaining option. None of the other treatments had worked. This was their last hope.

'At the moment you are only seeing in black and white. To you there is only living and dying, happiness or nothing.'

Something clicked as she realised what he was hinting at. A rush of anger forced her to her feet. 'No! You can't stop now. It's not like you. You're a fighter, you always have been. What you're saying now are the words of a quitter, of a coward!' Now she was breathing hard, the same fear that gripped her minutes before returned with such force, she thought it was going to consume her.

He looked at her with what she swore was pity. 'I know ya' don't understand. I wouldn't have myself, before all this happened. It's not that I am weak or a coward. In the last few months I've had to undergo countless surgeries and treatments, so don't think that I am scared to have one more. The truth is, is that I don't need to have that treatment. I don't need to fight this anymore.'

Clara couldn't believe what she was hearing. She began to pace the length of the room to stop herself from passing out as she began to shake. She couldn't lose him.

CATHRYN O'NEILL

'Please, come sit down so we can talk about this like adults, you are no longer that child that sat upon my knee.'

He spoke with a new found wisdom that Clara had never heard but it did nothing to calm her nerves.

'How can you do this? After everything we have been through, after everything we tried and promised each other. You do remember what you promised me, don't you?'

His expression was the only reply Clara needed. 'You said that you would fight this. You said that if you could survive the war then you could beat some silly old illness! Those were your words not mine.'

'Clara.'

Hearing her name stopped her in her tracks. For as long as she could remember he had never spoken to her as Clara. It was always Kid, Kiddo or even Chicken, but never Clara. She went and sat by his bed. She carefully picked up his hand, encasing it between hers.

'I don't want to lose you,' she whispered.

He sighed, obviously not wanting to have caused that reaction. 'You remember Nanny?'

Clara nodded. She was drained from the emotional cataclysm that rocked her body. She didn't move as the tear rolled down her cheek.

He slowly raised his hand and wiped it from her face as he spoke, his skin feeling like a fine sandpaper. 'Your Nanny was the most beautiful and caring person to ever walk this earth. And yet she was taken away at such an early age. For years I was angry at God. Angry that he took her away, and angry that he made her cross over and face the unknown without me. However, now I see that although she left without me, she wasn't alone.

'I beg of you, please do not hate God when I leave. Don't make the same mistake I did. I am leaving because I am ready. Before I can leave, I need to know you will not harbour any resentment. I need to know that you can move on and continue to live.'

Clara was silent. How did she not know he felt like this? How could one man keep his feelings hidden for so long? She opened her mouth to reply... nothing. She studied him, trying to find the answer. For the first time ever she looked at him and saw a broken man, a man who had finally come to terms with his emotions. Although he looked beaten, he still harboured a glimmer of hope. Clara guessed it was hope to see his departed wife again.

'I can hear her calling me, you know? When no one is here, or when I am alone in my dreams, I can hear Nanny calling me, telling me to come home.'

Clara finally understood that he was no longer holding on for himself, but for her. She softly chuckled as she comprehended the depth of his love for her; *he has fought off life's only definite to ensure I will be okay.*

He looked at her with a puzzled expression, obviously curious to her sudden mood swing.

'Pappy, I don't want you to hold on for me anymore. I want you to be happy, even if I can't be there to enjoy it with you. I can't lie, I will miss you tremendously, but I promise that I will continue to live without resentment. I love you.'

'I love you too, Kiddo.' Once again they embraced each other. Then they sat in silence. Clara watched as his strength began to slowly diminish. 'I think I'm gonna . . . .'

'It's okay Pappy, you can go to sleep if you want to.'

He smiled at her. She felt a new level of affection towards him, one that would outlive that of his life span. 'Goodnight, Kiddo.'

'Night Pappy.' She stayed for several more minutes, to make sure he was truly asleep before she left. His chest fell back into the irregular rise and fall. *Yes, he was still alive,* but Clara wondered how long it would be before his deteriorating breaths ceased to exist.

INSPIRED BY Alfred Lord Tennyson, *Crossing the Bar.*

ALPHA and OMEGA

2014 short stories
By Writers Anthology Group of the
Arts Alliance of Pine Rivers

ANGUISH
Brenda Simcox-Hunt

The sun sank gracefully behind the lea,
No one is here but he and me.
He turns and gazes into the open space
A puzzled frown across his beloved face.

'Why?' he asks, 'do you want to leave?'
Thinking, I paused, did not want to deceive.
'My trust has died, you have driven it away
By lying and cheating, I cannot stay.'

'Know I love you deep in my heart
I did not think we would ever part.'
'If you love me, why the other loves
You visit with gifts of gems and gloves?'

'I have this energy I must expend
Ladies are just a means to that end.
You are my life, my soul, my destiny
I cannot live without you beside me.'

Turning to look at me, his face is wet.
In his eyes I see anguish, and yet.
Could I love and forgive him once again?
To be his love, should I remain?

He tenderly pulls me to his manly chest.
My heart beats fast in my aching breast.
The time has come, I must decide
Go, or forever be by his side.

Through passing of time his cheating may wane
Then to me, he will be true again.
If I am calm and accept his ways
We can be happy all of our days.

INSPIRED BY Josephine's love for Napoleon

MICK'S EXODUS

Lach Thompson

GEORGE Street, Sydney CBD, February 23 1985, a time when pubs still had tiles on the walls outside and the men still pissed on them. The city was on the cusp of change, the first skirts were appearing in corner offices, the skyline was rising and the once sleepy streets were alight with new technology.

Change creates chances and when you're down on your luck finding the best odds becomes very important. And Mick Rowling was a man who would spend his short life seeking little more than a sure thing. We join him hunkered over a beer and sat at a bar, lit cigarette in one paw, a schooner cupped in the other.

The 22 year-old leaned back on his stool and squinted across the Great Southern Hotel. The smoke was thick and the bar was filled with the last few stragglers – the ones the publican let stay on after he shut the doors. The suited shoulders of the big end of town rubbed against the sweat stained shirts of those who'd spent a hot summer's day working in the sun. There wasn't a woman in sight.

Mick had only been in Sydney for one day. He'd set out in the farm ute his dad lent him, driving south along the Pacific Highway from Grafton, on Thursday. He arrived in the big smoke in the early hours of Friday morning. What followed was a relentless and panicked search for work. He'd rung up about every job in the paper, tried every trick and followed every lead and finally in the dying hours of the working week, Mr Rowling had secured gainful employment.

Come Monday he'd be selling ads in one of Kerry Packer's new magazines. The jaunt and the new job would be the first time he'd been away from his parents' cane farm, beside the Clarence River, for more than a month.

He swilled back the last few drops of his beer and reached for his wallet to buy another. And this was when it all began.

In the mad rush to get to his job interview Mick had forgotten to go to the bank and withdraw cash for the weekend and while he'd had his fill for the night, two days without money and nowhere to stay was a worrying prospect.

He pondered the problem. He could sleep on the tray of the ute but this wasn't Grafton and that didn't seem safe. Then he remembered the small square of plastic his mother, Jan, had given him just before he left.

'Now, you'll need a little money to get started but spend it wisely because we're not giving you more,' Jan had said.

'Joe at the bank says they have new machines that give you cash, in Sydney.

'You just punch in our postcode and tell it how much you want ... you've got $200.'

Mick's older brother had blown the kitty in that regard, when he tried to start out as a real estate agent in Brisbane. He'd lost the job after a week and stayed on for six months, returning home every weekend to claim more cash, before his parents pulled the plug. Now he was back working with the old man.

Mick took the small square of plastic from his wallet and looked at it – National Bank of Trust – it said in raised writing beside a tiny blue star. He beckoned the barman.

'Scuse me mate, do you know where I can use this?' he asked, waving the card.

'There's an ATM two blocks towards the Quay,' the barman replied pointing to his left.

Mick got up from his barstool, staggered out of the pub and turned left. The night had slipped away and when he'd entered the hotel the city's pavements had been full with smartly dressed, bustling folk on their way home to enjoy the weekend. Now it was just Mick, a few taxis and a hot northerly wind.

He walked for two blocks before seeing a National Bank of Trust. Next to the glassy sliding doors was a small steel box with a keypad on it. It was 11.51pm when Mick walked up and slipped the card into the machine. He punched in the postcode of his parents' farm and before he could think how much money he'd actually need he followed up by pressing the dollar sign and 200.

He waited a few moments and four clean $50 notes slid out. Mick folded them and went to walk away but he'd always been a chancer and he had a cheeky thought. He put the card back in the machine, put in the postcode and again entered $200. Moments later he was holding four more clean bills.

Mick paused and looked at his hand, he was holding $400, more money than he'd ever had. He looked back at the ATM and within seconds he was withdrawing another $200, then another and another. In the end he emptied the machine, it simply wouldn't take the card into the slot. In total he withdrew $4600, a lot of money in 1985.

You may not believe me but the following is a set of undeniable facts. In the mid 1980s, ATMs were a relatively new technology and they hadn't been perfected. There was one small glitch the National Bank of Trust hadn't ironed out. For ten minutes, from 11.50pm until midnight, some of the machines were offline and this left them unable to reach the bank's central system which told them how much money was in the accounts people were accessing. So the bank could continue to tell the public its ATMs were available 24 hours a day, during this 10-minute window the machines were simply wired to dispense a maximum of $200 in one hit.

Mick Rowling, the boy from a cane farm in the Clarence Valley, had stumbled upon a gold mine. His case and the facts surrounding it would set a precedent in the NSW Supreme Court that stands to this very day.

The question you have to ask yourself is this: if someone accidentally gives you something you're not entitled to, have you stolen it?

A BEARDED man walks down from a rocky crag in the desert. His people hunker before him, they are freed slaves, they are hungry, their faith is wavering but they know he has a message. And the 42nd sentence he said to them that day, as they kneeled in the Egyptian sand, would become Exodus 22:7:

'If a man gives to his neighbor money or goods to keep safe, and it is stolen from the man's house, then, if the thief is found, he shall pay double.'

___oOo___

IT WAS 11am. Mick ripped the waxy paper of the $3000 antique bible he'd bought at Barsby's – Sydney's finest auction house – just three days earlier. He took care not to tear any of the words out. Instead he stuck firmly to the margins. Once he'd ripped out a large piece of paper he folded it and dumped in a small handful of pot. He rolled a very large joint, lit it and walked across his spacious open-plan living room. The garden balcony of his top-floor apartment, on Kirribilli Avenue, looked straight out at the Opera House Circular Quay spanned out before him, glistening beneath a blue sky and the tall buildings of Sydney rose behind it. He took a long heavy toke on his spliff and thought it was as if the whole city were literally at his feet.

It was winter 1986 and in the past year and four months Mick Rowling had gone from country-boy nobody to being Sydney's hottest mystery man. He'd worked just two days as an ad rep before hitting another ATM. He'd waited a week dreading a call from home, but when none came he went back again. He'd waited another week, dreading a call from the police, before he did it again. Each time he emptied the ATM, taking about $5000.

He didn't know why it worked, or why no one had raised an alarm, all he knew was that if you went to any National Bank of Trust ATM at

11.51pm on a Friday you could withdraw as much money as you liked and no one would notice. He'd opened new accounts, deposited next to nothing in them and taken out more ATM cards. He'd pay friends to empty other ATMs in all corners Sydney – making out like they were running an errand to get him cash.

Under his bed were bundles of $50 notes. He'd never counted them but in total he had more than $200,000.

He'd imported a new Porsche from Germany and it sat downstairs in his private garage, beside a small collection of Triumph motorcycles. He'd bought a wardrobe of tailored suits, shirts and ties from Rochefort's, on Elizabeth Street. He'd purchased designer casual clothes from Gucci, Armani and Hugo Boss. He'd spent thousands on cobbler made boots of stiff, brown English leather. At home he wore Japanese silk dressing gowns and he had a stand with fifteen hats made by Sydney's finest milliner next to his front door. Even his silk handkerchiefs were worth $50 each and he was always trying to give them to a beautiful woman.

He spent his days between the races at Randwick, sunbathing at Bondi Beach and drinking and dining at Sydney's finest eateries. He had a running tab at the Berowra Waters Inn and regularly caught a water taxi across to Rose Bay before flying in a seaplane to eat at the secluded restaurant on Middle Harbour. Rockpool Bar and Grill had just opened its doors and Mick Rowling was their best customer. He'd regularly walk in and order a bottle of Don Perignon and two-dozen oysters.

He'd cleared the mortgage on the old farm and bought his parents a house by sea, in Yamba, on the New South Wales North Coast. They thought he'd made it big in advertising, others thought he was a drug dealer – no one knew the truth.

Then there were the women. Since discovering his secret he'd never been without one. It was amazing how charming a man became when he was young, good-looking, down to earth and inexplicably very rich. He'd walk into one of the city's finest establishments and shout the whole bar, then pick the prettiest girl and whisk her off to the top floor of the Shangri La where he paid the Hotel staff a retainer to make him cocktails, 24 hours a day.

There was one woman who'd risen above the others; a pretty, blonde journalist Mick had met during a blurred night at a pool party in Vaucluse. Her name was Harper and he'd bought her a five-carat diamond ring. They were in love and engaged to be married but Mick was frequently unfaithful.

He'd made many fast friends and those new acquaintances had introduced him to drugs - which he loved. He'd sink into warm numbness after smoking heroin, soar high on the sharp invincibility of cocaine, or embrace the pure joy of ecstacy almost every night.

Mick Rowling was free from the chains of commerce, the enslavement of money that had kept his father at work in the cane fields, his hands calloused and cracked, his brow sunburnt and beat. Mick pitied his father and feared no man. He was a freed slave.

THEY were hungry and fearful, but they were free from the Pharaoh. Their backs bore the scars of their former master's whips. Their spirits were all but broken, yet on that day they were awestruck. For every man and women there knew, the words Moses was muttering in the desert would change the world. They were: Exodus 21: 24 to 27:

'Eye for eye, tooth for tooth, hand for hand, foot for foot, burning for burning, wound for wound, stripe for stripe.

And if a man smite the eye of his servant, or the eye of his maid, that it perish; he shall let him go free for his eye's sake.'

FROM age 12 Teddy Fullerton had known his life would be great. He'd always been the smartest boy in his class. He'd been educated at one of

Sydney's finest private schools and captained the first XV in year 10. While the other families lived on the stuffy North Shore his father bought a mansion overlooking Freshwater Beach. Every morning when the wind was offshore, he'd surf and he surfed better than anyone he knew.

By the time he was 32-years old he was the Chairman of the Board of one of the country's most lucrative investment banks. He'd made a fortune. And by the time he was 34 he was the Minister for Police and Emergency Services. On November 3 1986 he was sitting at a table in the Sydney Club, across the road from the Parliament of New South Wales. Across from him were the CEO of the National Bank of Trust, the Police Commissioner and a pretty young publicist named Penny.

They were working out how to solve a vexing problem.

'The legal advice from the Crown Solicitor is unclear, we're not even sure if it is larceny,' Teddy said.

'And I have to say the press would be very bad, this does nothing to ensure confidence in the banks, or the police.'

'Are we sure we can't just ignore this?'

Noel Piguet had led a life of privilege not too dissimilar to Teddy, except he was part of the Melbourne set and a far less impressive man. He was 54-years old and very thin with white hair and glasses. There was a large bald patch on the crown of his head. He was the CEO of the National Bank of Trust. He'd gotten to where he was by attacking the credibility of those around him. Most people were fooled by his act - they thought he was nice. Those close to him, including his wife and children knew he was quietly a little incompetent and very weak.

'Teddy, we have been ignoring the vast majority of these withdrawals,' he said anxiously.

'And we would have kept ignoring them, to save the press and because they're mostly accidental, but this one fellow seems to have worked it out.

'We think he's withdrawn almost half a million dollars but we can't be sure because the machines are offline when it happens.'

Police Commissioner Nigel Wrathstone was one of the most hated men in New South Wales. Obviously the crooks hated him, but so did most police. He was seen as a blow-in, an English import, cherry picked from Scotland Yard.

Without the support of Teddy Fullerton there was no way he could have kept his job. Every day for Nigel was a constant battle but at 42 he was a man on top of his game, a man of formidable integrity with a lot of backbone. He and Teddy hated Piguet – privately they would come to call him the jellyfish: spineless, brainless and transparent.

'The bank's role in all this will have to be investigated,' Nigel said.

'I don't think it would be appropriate for us to discuss this any further.

'Have a good night.'

Teddy and Nigel looked over towards the big double cedar-doors that lead into the Sydney Club's dining room. Nigel got up awkwardly and left the room.

His dessert – a bombe Alaska – would arrive a few minutes later. In the end the waiter would eat it.

Six months later Noel would be sacked after documents showing his knowledge of the unsanctioned withdrawals were leaked to the media by Teddy.

In 1990 Teddy would be forced to resign over deals he cut with the North Sydney banking set in return for electoral donations.

Nigel now lives on a farm in Gloucestshire, England. He left Australia after being hounded by more or less every journalist in Sydney. He privately tells anyone who will listen Australians are the most vulgar, backward people in the world.

While all three men led exceptional lives they were never free of problems, they were rich and powerful but never carefree. When they read the story of Mick Rowling in the papers, they were all secretly very jealous. Deep down they all knew they were enslaved.

The Daily Clarion September 5 1988, page 5
Brett Meer

NOTORIOUS fraudster Mick Rowling has been found dead in his cell, in Silverwater Jail.

Rowling, 25, gained national attention three years ago when it was revealed he had illegally withdrawn more than half a million dollars from ATMs across Sydney.

While on a crazed spending spree he developed something of a public profile, becoming particularly well known in racing circles.

At the time of his arrest Rowling was engaged to former gossip columnist, Harper McDermott.

Yesterday, Ms McDermott declined to comment on her former lover's untimely death. However, she was photographed visiting Rowling's family home near Grafton, in northern New South Wales.

Ms McDermott was sacked from her position with Goss and Glam after NSW Police revealed she had given cash Rowling had taken from the National Bank of Trust to Queen's Counsel Glenn Bruisemann. No formal charges have ever been laid against her.

Rowling gained folk-hero status after he beat the first round of charges police brought against him, in the Supreme Court of NSW.

His barrister, Mr Bruisemann, successfully argued he could not be found guilty because he honestly believed he had a right to the money he withdrew.

He was later stripped of his assets and found guilty of larceny after the NSW State Government amended the Crimes Act.

An investigation by *The Daily Clarion* revealed disgraced National Bank of Trust CEO, Noel Piguet had deliberately concealed the glitch in the bank's ATM network which enabled Rowling to make the illegal withdrawals.

Documents published by this newspaper showed he had concealed the issue from his board out of fear the bank's failure to solve the problem would cost him his job.

NSW Police Minister, Teddy Fullerton told *The Daily* the death was not being treated as suspicious.

'Every death in custody is a tragedy and an investigation into Mr Rowling's death will be undertaken by Correctional Services,' he said.

'I understand there was evidence of narcotic use at the scene.'

The Daily understands Mr Rowling scrawled the words 'Chosen One' on the wall of his cell, in his own feces, in the hours before his death.

Serendipity

Arts Alliance Anthology

Arts Alliance Anthology

2013 Anthology

BETRAYAL
Brenda Simcox-Hunt

Bright shines the sun on the dew soaked grass
Peace surrounds me.
High in the hills, snow covers the pass,
I wait for him.

The wind ruffles my hair, a playful breeze.
Birds sing songs of praise.
Amongst the wild flowers, sheep contentedly graze.
He comes not.

Dark clouds creep menacingly over the hill,
A feeling of foreboding enfolds me.
I see him walking beside a nearby rill
Hand in hand he walks with HER.

My world falls apart.

INSPIRED BY dreams

CATHRYN O'NEILL

THE PRE-NUP

Raelene Purtill

'I SHOULD have kissed you.' St. John stood in the vestry waiting with the bride.

She turned from her last minute make-up touches. 'What?'

He retreated. 'I'm sorry did I say that out loud?'

'When should you have kissed me?'

'Before today. Before all this.' He indicated the decorated church and the guests seated patiently, murmuring in polite anticipation of the coming nuptials.

'Kiss me now.' She moved toward him. Her fragrance was inviting but he said,

'I can't. Not like I want to.'

'Then kiss me like I want you to.' She was backing him up into the dresser.

'How's that?'

'Like a friend wishing me well on my wedding day.'

'I know you would have kissed me back,' he stammered.

'No, St. John.' She shook her head, so close to him now the little curly ringlets from under her veil brushed his face. 'It's always been Edward.'

As she pushed her face toward him to meet his cheek, he turned his head and met her lips with his own. Cupping her face, he held it close. All the years of friendship were now something else. She pulled away from him with her hands pressed to her cheeks.

'I knew you'd kiss me back.' He grinned.

She paced to the window. 'All this time and I never knew. Today of all days, you make me choose.'

'There's no choice, Jane. You will marry Edward.'

'What about us?'

St. John scoffed. 'There was never any us. It's always been Edward, as you said.'

St. John turned to make his way from the vestry and enter the church.

'Don't leave me St. John.'

At the sound of her voice, he came close again. 'I am leaving you Jane. I leave you and your faithless heart to the man you deserve.'

'I don't understand.'

'It hasn't always been Edward, has it? I just proved a point.'

'So you kissed her like that to prove a point?' Edward entered the vestry.

'Don't . . . '

'It's okay Jane. What point was that, Rivers?'

'You are both as fickle as each other. And you, you . . . .' St. John punctuated the sentence with his index finger.

'Ignore him, Jane. Come on.' They turned to enter the church. St. John followed.

'Hey, Edward perhaps I should have kissed you!'

'You slimy bastard.' Edward turned and leapt. He landed in the aisle with St. John beneath him.

'You take that back.' His heavy fist found its mark.

'Get off me.' St. John tasted blood in his mouth.

'Do you yield?' It was a question that carried their childhood and all their years of friendship with it. During the pause that followed, St. John searched Edward's face for truth. The gaze remained steady and St. John had his answer. Rochester would be faithful. Jane was forgiven.

'I yield. Now get off me so we can get on with this wedding.'

The congregation once again in its place, St. John moved to his position at the front of the church speaking through his cut lip. 'Dear friends we are gathered here today . . .'

_____ooo_____

ST. John Rivers shook his head to remove the memory and touched his lip which had felt both joy and pain that wedding day. Here, now taking tea at the Synod, he was among his peers. Men of the cloth whose own experiences of love might weigh as heavily as his. He hid behind his tea cup as one of them approached him.

'How do you do, Mr Rivers? Have I told you how my patron, the Lady Catherine de Burgh has sponsored me to this synod?' St. John's smile mirrored that of the greasy, fawning man before him.

In the same tone he replied, 'I myself am here at the pleasure of the Rochesters. Mr Edward and my cousin, Jane, have graciously paid my lodgings.'

He sipped more tea while the bore continued. *Peers my foot.*

'Ah. Yes I have heard about your cousin Jane. I understand she worked as a governess for Mr Rochester and that there was some scandal on their wedding day. I must say Lady Catherine de Burgh would never stand for such...'

That was it. Scandal be damned.

'And you Mr Collins are easily distracted. You would marry Miss Jane Bennett and upon her being unavailable your eyes quickly turned to Miss Elizabeth who summarily rejected you.'

Collins padded his brow with a handkerchief and ducked his head. 'And you, Mr Rivers. Your Jane did not take to the idea of being a missionary's wife.' He tucked the handkerchief in his pocket with a flurry and watched St. John for a reply.

'I take heart Mr Collins that she was not averse to being a missionary.'

'Just not with you, heh?' It was almost under his breath, but St. John heard it.

He was not going to be drawn into this by some rural parson unable to make his own way in the world.

'No. Not with me by her side. You are correct.'

But Collins also backed away from any real confrontation.

'It seems Mr Rivers we are one in that circumstance; placing our affections where they are not wanted.'

That was true enough. St. John nodded and, having finished his drink, placed the cup on the trolley beside him, looking to end to this conversation.

'Well, I am on my way to India all the same. I shall seek comfort in my Lord and Saviour.' He folded his arms in front of him, while Collins continued.

'That is noble, Mr Rivers. Lady Catherine de Burgh has assured me her sponsorship shall only continue lest I marry to her approval.'

'You have I see. Charlotte Lucas is quite the reverend's wife.' He nodded towards the little woman conversing with other wives near the window. She glanced their way and nodded before returning her attention to her group. Collins chest expanded. *Prideful too*, St. John noted.

'Yes. We are comfortable,' Collins said. 'I do admire you Mr Rivers, continuing to India alone.'

'While you are to be at the beck and call of your sponsor? I believe her to be a more harsh employer than our own Almighty.'

'As you say, Mr Rivers. As you say.'

I LOVE stories with clergy in them, such things as *The Thornbirds* or *I Heard the Owl call my Name*. I chose here for the anthology theme, Pride and Prejudice and Jane Eyre.

Both Mr Collins and St. John Rivers were unlucky in love, although Mr Collins pursued various women until he met his match.

While Jane Austen (1775-1817) and Charlotte Bronte (1816-1855) were years apart, I thought it would be fun to put these characters together to discuss their relationships.

– Raelene Purtill

ENI AND MEENI

Francis E J Beecher

LITTLE eyes opened and looked around to find that there were others who looked just the same, for indeed they also had just been born. Well it was a bit of a struggle but somehow, not long thereafter, everyone was munching on a nice juicy leaf and the struggle seemed forgotten.

It seemed so natural to just hop right in and have a good feed. It was great but after a while a stop seemed in order. Looking around, to my surprise, I saw only one other. *Where did they all go?* He thought.

'Perhaps I should introduce myself? But, I don't know my name? I don't even know if I am a boy or a girl.' Let's say *he*. Of course he also did not know he was 'the Gardener's Curse' either for he was a caterpillar. Can you tell if a caterpillar is a boy or girl? *I know. I shall call myself 'Eni'. Yes I like that,* he thought.

So Eni went and introduced himself to the other caterpillar. 'I know we have not been introduced,' Eni said, 'but my name is Eni and I thought that as we are neighbours it would be good for us to be friends.'

Well of course just like Eni the other caterpillar did not know that all the others had gone for it had been so busy having a really good feed.

Also just like Eni the other caterpillar did not know anything about boy or girl stuff. And yes, you're right, did not even have a name. It was however rather frightened and blurted out, 'My name is Meeni.' This was because he really had no idea of a name and it sounded like Eni.

Meeni felt so proud of having thought of a name so quickly and invited Eni to have some of the lovely cabbage leaf Meeni had been feasting upon. It seemed no time at all, although it was hours really when they both felt so full it seemed only polite to stop eating, for a little while at least, and so they began to chat to each other.

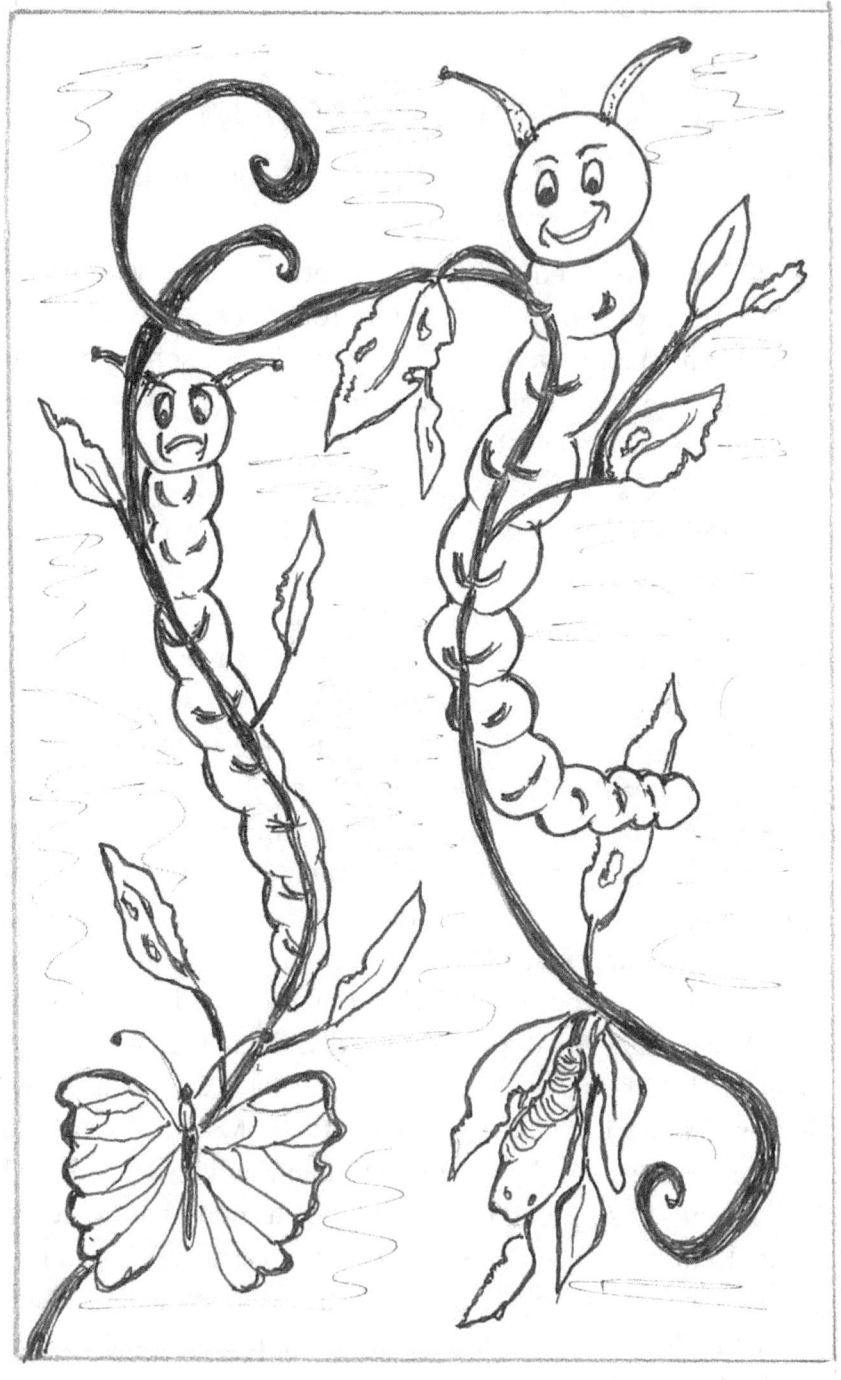

Eni found Meeni interesting but very nervous. Frightened of every flutter of a leaf, altogether a timid soul, Eni thought. At the same time Meeni thought, rather enviously, that Eni was so brave and confident.

Days passed in much the same way and Eni and Meeni were growing (as caterpillars do) so very quickly. Eni had been looking around and thinking, turning to Meeni he said, 'I think we may be attracting some attention, for what with all the excellent food we have had here, the garden is getting a bit ragged don't you think?'

Meeni was frightened and told Eni how everything was so lovely and if he really was his friend he would not say such things.

Eni told Meeni of all the adventures Eni was sure were waiting for them if only they would 'have a go' as Eni said.

It was no use trying to persuade Meeni. Eni was saddened by Meeni's responses for deep down Eni knew that something was just passing them by.

Eni felt all the adventures of life were waiting and although he was also frightened of leaving, Eni was also frightened of losing the friendship of the only friend he had ever known. It was a feeling deep inside him that there were adventures waiting, places and things he could not even begin to imagine, and he was now prepared, and ready to take on the world.

Though Eni did not even know what the world was or what may happen, 'I have to try' was a thought that would not leave Eni's head.

Meeni tried all sorts of emotional blackmail that made it so hard for Eni, but in the end Eni with a heavy heart told Meeni he felt he was prepared and had to go.

The two friends gave each other a great big hug. Meeni did not want to let Eni go and Eni had to tear himself from Meeni's arms. So it was early one morning Eni left the garden to see the world and have some adventures. Eni did not really know what an adventure was but it seemed to cheer him up whenever he thought of it. Of course Eni was frightened and thought it might be prudent (that means a good idea) to try and keep out of sight as much as possible for everything was new and Eni did not know any hiding places any more.

The fact that a caterpillar has very sun-sensitive skin and would make a lovely meal for a hungry bird of course would not even have entered Eni's mind (You think? Hmm.)

Eni travelled by night and hid during the day for Eni found there were lots and lots of things with just no manners, who only just wanted to eat him.

Eni met plenty of different kinds of people but never found anyone like Meeni. By now with all the variety of foods that Eni had been able to find on the adventures Eni had grown quite large, well alright how about we settle for big. Ginormous in fact and that is big even by caterpillar standards. But as everyone would tell you Eni was so well mannered.

Everyone who met Eni was absolutely charmed by Eni's grace and eloquence for Eni had grown to be quite an authority on so many of the weighty matters that seemed to fill the lives of those he met. Indeed Eni's advice was sought out by a wide variety these days.

Eni thought of his friend Meeni from time to time even though Eni had such a full life on his travels. One day Eni found it so hard to stay awake, feeling very sleepy. What Eni did not know was that if a caterpillar lives long enough they have a secret way in which they can change into a butterfly.

Eni felt that it had been such a little while ago that Eni had left his friend Meeni but Eni was feeling soo, soo sleepy. It seemed Eni could not think about much these days. So it was that Eni wrapped himself into a cocoon, (that is like wrapping a blanket tightly around yourself and hiding from everything and everyone.)

Well Eni must have remembered the secret way to become a butterfly for what did not seem a long time. Eni could be seen sunning and drying out a pair or the finest wings you could ever wish to see. Well there would be no more unkind words like 'Slob' from those envious ones over there Eni thought.

Lillian Tebescoff
E M g Meeni

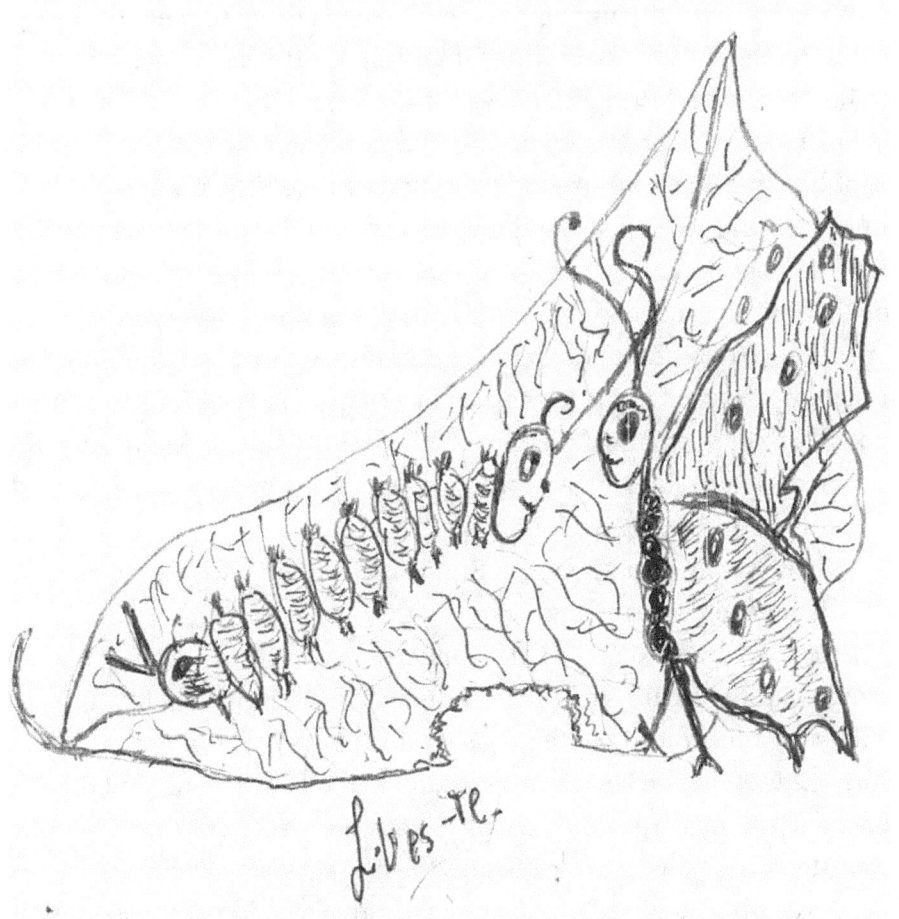

Libes-te,

It is one thing to have wings but quite another to know what to do with them! So Eni had quite a few misadventures, bumping into people and all sorts of things before Eni got the hang of this wonderful new adventure of flying.

That's fair enough too, for even you and I have to practice something before we can say we have got the hang of it, don't we?

So it was that Eni came to fly. It seemed no sooner did he get comfortable with the new wings than Eni felt this overwhelming urge to find Meeni and the garden where they were born.

This was not easy, for Eni found that being now so light the wind kept blowing Eni, and usually (of course, wouldn't you know it) to all the wrong places. Eni was quite determined and so it was one day that Eni was looking over the garden that was so fondly remembered, (as one of Eni's friends had remarked) 'when Eni was only a grub.'

The garden now though looked absolutely dreadful, and much to Eni's surprise he saw his friend Meeni was in a bad way. Skin and bone poor thing thought Eni, rushing to his friend's side trying to hide the shock of seeing Meeni lying there in such an awful way. Dreadful, dreadful kept echoing in Eni's head.

It took only a moment for Eni to realise that Meeni was close to death, not even recognising Eni at first.

Eni explained to Meeni the wonderful adventures and how come a new beautiful figure and these wonderful wings which Eni flapped wildly for Meeni to see. Meeni gave one last look at Eni and said how sorry he was that he had been so frightened to go with Eni, and that his life had been miserable, just trying to keep body and soul together. That was Meeni's final words for Meeni's life had slipped away.

Whoosh, Eni heard and instinctively ducked sideways just in time to miss the gardener's net. With no time to think about a friend now Eni flew high and soon found that with a little help (this time) from the wind, why there below was another lovely garden.

So it was that as evening fell Eni was tucked behind a large leaf watching the stars come out, thinking of the times now long past when growing up, preparing and dreaming of adventures, and it had all happened. All those wonderful people, and places, Eni felt so very fortunate, lucky that's what I was! *Caterpillar goodness gracious*, he thought, do you know how many pairs of shoes a caterpillar wears out. *Why, however did I manage?* Eni thought.

Stars watched Eni smile at the end of a long adventurous day, watching as a dream carried those sleepy eyes at last to sleep. I wonder what Eni will be doing when in the morning a new day peeks out from the night sky, who knows what or where the next adventure will be, now that it seems Eni has those beautiful new wings under control?

If only I could be a passenger on Eni's wings to see all the places and share in the adventures that Eni's new life will bring. Flying through the air, as light as a feather, that would be really magical, wouldn't it? Tell me what do you think?

CATHRYN O'NEILL

THE DOG WALKER

Bakthi Ross

MASON walked with his dog, never missed a day. He stopped at the same rock and he sat down admiring nature while his dog was free to roam the bush. When the dog finished his daily routine it came back and scratched the grass and wagged its tail indicating it was ready to go home. Mason tapped his walking stick on the rock and stood up and put on the dog leash. They both walked the same path home.

Mrs Brown everyday watched Mason walking with his little terrier. She rarely went out to say hello to Mason. It was as if Mrs Brown's time was planned to certain events to happen in a day. Even though Mason was a stranger, when he was on holiday and did not walk the dog, everyone felt their day's routine was spoiled. All the things had to happen in order or they will talk. Mrs Brown runs to the lady next door, her name is Marion and tells her Mason didn't walk the dog today. Marion goes and tells another. By the end of the evening Mrs Brown gets the message Mason had gone on a holiday. He won't be back for a couple of weeks. She is unsettled and waits for Mason to come back.

Mrs Brown sits near the window and watches the day go by but is unsettled and misses Mason and the terrier.

Everyone has to be calm and day's events have to happen in same order or it will be panic among the window watchers. Two weeks went by without Mason and his dog.

When he came back Mrs Brown, after sitting and watching them all these years, decided to talk to Mason. She went outside interrupted his routine walk and said 'hello.' Even though she knew he had been on holiday she said to him, 'I haven't seen you for a while.'

The big conversation happened between them. Mason introduced himself and talked about the details of his life and about his holiday and the pitfalls of society. They stood and talked for hours, after which they knew each other's business in detail. A serious invasion of privacy but they both did not feel that way even though they met for the first time. Mason established a trust in Mrs Brown. They talked as if they had known each other for years. An exchange of telephone numbers and he asked her to come for lunch next week at his home. Mrs Brown was accepted by the terrier. Usually it barked its head off when anyone came near Mason. Finally they said, 'See you next week at lunch time,' and walked away in different directions.

Mrs Brown blushed and smiled.

Mason thought about her curiously and talked to his dog and said, 'She is coming for lunch next week, you better behave yourself.' Whether it was intended for himself or the dog was in doubt.

Mrs Brown went home and looked at herself in the mirror like a teenage girl. Feeling old and having lost that spark in her face, she applied lipstick. She was a bit hyped up. She looked at her wardrobe and thought which dress should she wear for the lunch. I do not want to look too excited. I better keep myself calm, she talked to herself.

The next few days Mason walked the dog but Mrs Brown was reluctant to go and talk to him. She saved herself for that special lunch. She couldn't stop thinking about him. After all these years a first lunch with someone. Then she thought about her past husband, 'He would be happy for me,' she said. She laughed looking at herself in the mirror. 'Oh! I am being silly.' For so many lonely days she had sat at that window, and on that same old chair, and watched the world go by. Every day was same: nothing exciting happened for her. If her chair had a mouth it would tell all about her feelings. Her fiddly crafts, home magazines and knitting were all that occupied her. After a little conversation with Mason she totally lost her focus. Everything seemed meaningless. She lost interest in knitting. Still, that happy blushing on her face, she couldn't wipe it off.

The special day arrived. Mrs Brown didn't sleep well the night before. She got up early and dressed herself and waited for that exact time. The clock moved more slowly than usual.

She walked out the door and went to Mason's house, with its giant French door with a welcome sign. She rang the bell. Mason opened the door and welcomed her in. A kiss on the cheek from him reassured all the imagination she had had for the past week. Mrs Brown looked around Mason's house, beautifully decorated and she suspected a lady must have involved. He couldn't have done it all by himself, she thought. A lady with a tray of tea and cakes entered the room. Mason said, 'This is Felma, my house keeper, she comes in every Wednesday.' Mrs Brown was relieved.

A young good looking housekeeper, no, I cannot be jealous about her, thought Mrs Brown. I am not pretty like her. If Mason hasn't fallen for her, what chance would I have, she asked herself. She kept herself calm. The housekeeper served the tea and left the room.

Mason took a sip of the tea. Mrs Brown took a sip of the tea. Words did not flow between. Mason brought in the photo album with photos of all his family memories and his travels. He was seriously interested in travelling. That was how their conversation started. A settled down man and settled down woman looking to rekindle the youth in themselves. Nothing happened between them. A photo album and a good lunch, they had. A good wine didn't evoke anything. They both were in that comfort zone and couldn't give up that style of life to go into new adventures. So they settled for enjoying lunch and talk. With the red wine they talked and talked all sorts of things. That special lunch was over.

Her lonely days without her husband were over. She sat at that window and watched Mason walking the dog again. Mrs Brown was inspired by his dedication to his dog. Mason and she travelled together and had lunches but continued their separate lives.

They took a cruise on the River Nile. Both dressed like Arabs and enjoyed their time together. But their conversations seemed to die down too quickly. They both were holding on to something and didn't let go. They came down to breakfast, lunch and dinner on the cruise like any other travelers. While they were eating they were watching others more than talking between themselves. A river like the Nile ran a long way but their relationship seemed to be ended with the cruise. They were bored. None of his conversation suited Mrs Brown. The view from her home window had had more birds and bees.

They ate and enjoyed the entertainment on the cruise but once you are accustomed to a type of life, change looks hard. They were both limited in their conversations and sometimes they repeated themselves. Mrs Brown thought, I'd better go back to my magazines. *My story characters have more life than this.* On the way home they didn't talk much at all. A silence of a kind overpowered their heads and they showed boredom.

They got off the cruise and went home. Mrs Brown didn't ring him or visit him again. She got back to her chair and read and did craft. Whenever Mason walked the dog she watched him and thought he loved that dog and its company. His dog is more important than people to him. Why she became so secluded she didn't know.

What she looked for in others was not there anymore. A long time being alone made her like that. Her own company and the things she did for fun were more important to her. Being away from her window she felt she missed that space and her garden with flowers. She fed some birds on her window sill. The birds' chirps and their dedication to coming for their seeds made her happy. Mrs Brown sometimes sang songs of her past to the birds. Some songs stayed in her memory and she could sing them without any music.

The birds listened and flew here and there on the window. She was the closed flower which only blossomed once. Some trees do not re-shoot. They die down gracefully.

THE THREE LEGIONNAIRES

R. William Penshorn

HANDSOME twenty-five year old survey draftsman, Ray Williams was in love with beautiful twenty-two year old Cherie Dale and she too with him, or so he thought until she met up with debonair millionaire movie producer Zane Black. Zane was more than twice Cherie's age and recently divorced. When he met Cherie, who was a budding actress, he was infatuated by her youthful beauty. He offered her stardom if she agreed to do things his way.

Zane was as smooth as glass and soon had Cherie eating out of his hand. She fell for him like a ton of bricks and soon put an end to her romance with Ray Williams. Ray was in disbelief and heartbroken.

During that same time, Brian John, a man in his late twenties, worked in sales for Arnold Simpson's advertising company. Brian was disillusioned with his life. Nothing ever seemed to go right.

He tried without success to learn to play a musical instrument. He joined a cycling club and a swimming club but could never satisfy himself with his performances. He was fond of the opposite sex and thought if he learned to dance he might have a chance at getting to know some of them but alas, he had two left feet and that too became another failure to add to his list.

One night at a bar with a friend named Stan, he noticed a very attractive woman constantly staring at him. Stan egged him on to approach her and invite her for a drink with him.

After some friendly persuasion, Brian reluctantly did so and was delighted when the woman agreed to. Her name was Robin. She was twenty-five years old.

They became a couple and went out on dates where they would carry out some heavy petting. It was not long before Brian plucked up enough courage to invite Robin to his bedroom. When she eagerly agreed, Brian was ecstatic.

Brian felt as though a bomb had been dropped at his feet when in the privacy of his bedroom, Robin began to undress to reveal in actual fact, 'she' was male. Brian began to dry retch. 'I thought you knew I was a man,' Robin uttered in a weak voice. That was the end of that.

Brian's career was at an all-time low at that time. He was currently working to gain a contract with the very wealthy MacTaggart Industries. His boss, Arnold Simpson, warned him if Mactaggarts did not go along with his ideas, he would be looking for another job. The project did not eventuate. Brian was jobless and at his wits' end.

Also around that period of time, a ruggedly handsome forty-year-old man named Neville Keith was working as a driller for the Texas Geophysical Survey Company. The contract he was employed on was in its final days. The camp boss, Texan Bill Tancher, offered Neville work on a new project in Alaska. That sounded a bit too cool for Neville. He thanked Bill and decided to take a break and go to spend a bit of time in Las Vegas.

While there, enjoying a winning spree on a roulette wheel at Circus-Circus Casino, he was confronted by a pretty dark-eyed Italian woman who introduced herself as Julie Nucifora. Neville told Julie he was in between jobs. She was staying at the Circus-Circus Hotel. After a few more successful spins, Julie invited Neville to her room. He did not need to be asked twice.

To his surprise when they arrived in her room, they were met by two Italian men who turned out to be Julie's cousins. They were Roberto and Rosso who also went by the Nucifora name.

They offered Neville a generous sum of money that made his Casino winnings look like chicken feed, to drive a Ford Fairlane with a certain cargo in the trunk to an address in Los Angeles.

Neville smelled a rat and asked why they would not want to do it themselves. They replied he would be better off if he was unaware of certain facts. The amount of cash was greater than Neville would make in more than two years. He decided to go ahead with the deal. Julie said she would go along as passenger as she had unfinished business in Los Angeles herself.

During the drive, Neville noticed a green Buick Wildcat was following at a distance for the entire journey. Upon arriving at the address, he and Julie were greeted by several thugs. The green Buick pulled in behind him. Two men disembarked from it, guns drawn. One called out, 'FBI, don't any of you move'. One of the thugs took out a pistol and fired at the FBI agents. Everyone ducked for cover. Neville made a run for it, jumped a couple of fences and kept on going.

Around about that time, two pretty English sisters, Melanie and Niki Bird, were taking a bus tour through France. It was mid-afternoon when the bus pulled up for a one hour stop in at a small village about one hour away from Paris.

Like the other passengers, the girls went for a walk. When it was time to return to the bus to continue on their way, the girls did not show up. The police were notified but the girls were not found. Their whereabouts remained a mystery.

The girls were captured by men on the payroll of a terrorist leader named Ahab Saddam. They were flown to his desert head-quarters which was an elaborate camp by an oasis with pleasant surroundings somewhere in North Africa. They were to be placed in his harem as love slaves. They were infuriated.

Johanna, the princess of the slave girls, warned Melanie and Niki there was no escape. All who had tried in the past had been shot.

Ahab Saddam was most pleased with the English girls upon their arrival. He laughed at their resistance to his advances and would say, 'I need not worry, time is on my side.'

Saddam's terrorist camp was approximately fifty miles across the desert from a Foreign Legion Fort that was under the rule of Commander Andre Jordan. The same day as the girls arrived at Saddam's camp, three American men stood before Commander Jordan to be enlisted as Legionnaires. They were, Ray Williams, Brian John and Neville Keith.

The men were shown to their quarters. While unpacking, a short wave radio news message stated that the daughters of a British Earl had mysteriously gone missing, last seen at a small village not far from Paris. 'It'd be nice to hear some good news for a change,' said Brian.

'Yeh, like the happening of the Second Coming,' Neville replied.

'Yeh, something like that.' Ray agreed, followed by a chuckle.

A thick set rugged faced Irish man made his way to talk to the new comers with two mean-faced men close behind him. 'I'm Bill Maguire. They call me 'Bull'. This is just to let you know that I'm the boss around here. Do things my way and you'll stay outta trouble. Get it?'

Ray rolled his eyes. Neville and Brian nodded politely for the sake of keeping the peace.

A few nights later at dinner time in the mess hall, Brian was carrying a tray with three bowls of soup to the table where he sat with his companions. Bull stuck his foot in the way to trip Brian. Soup went everywhere. Brian quietly told Bull it was his fault and insisted he cleaned it up. 'Clean it up yourself you clumsy idiot,' Bull snapped, clenching his fists. 'Didn't I tell you I'm the bloody boss around here?'

'Clean it up,' Brian said quietly.

Bull pulled back his fist ready to punch Brian in his jaw when Ray hastily stood and demanded Bull clean it up himself. Bull told him to mind his own business when Commander Jordan entered the mess hall. 'What's going on?' he demanded.

'No need for concern Sir. Bull had a little mishap with the soup and was about to clean it up weren't you Bull?' said Ray.

'Er yes,' Bull mumbled and proceeded to clean up the mess.

Commander Jordan announced to the Legionnaires a warning of an imminent attack by Saddam's terrorists had leaked to him. 'We will get them first and take them by surprise,' he said. 'Prepare to leave in convoy ready to attack first thing in the morning.'

Before leaving the following morning, the Commander informed the Legionnaires he had just received further word that Saddam's forces were already on their way. He ordered his convoy to set up in ambush at Wilma Pass, a narrow roadway through a range of huge rocks ranging to three hundred and fifty feet high.

His patrols lost no time in doing so. Ray, Brian and Neville were in charge of a covered truck carrying ammunition including bazookas and a sub machine gun mounted at the rear.

Saddam did not go into battle. He put leadership of that in the hands of his second in charge, Abdul Khayam. Saddam stayed in the camp with his harem. He explained to Johanna it would be silly for a successful man such as himself to be in the battlefield when he could relax in the camp and enjoy the pleasures life had to offer.

Melanie and Niki swam in a clear pool. Both were clad in bikinis. 'This would be quite pleasurable if it were somewhere else,' Niki said. 'How I would love to get out of this God forsaken place.'

Marlena, a very attractive long haired blonde who was also a slave girl was in the pool with them. She overheard the sisters and told them guard duty was considerably reduced when the battles were being fought and if there was any chance to escape, then would be the time.

Saddam's 4WD Overlander was parked outside his tent. He always carried the key to it on his belt. He was currently in his tent with Johanna. Orders not to be disturbed had been issued. Melanie and Niki left the pool.

'Good luck,' Marlena whispered.

The sisters made their way toward Saddam's tent. They passed by a sleeping-quarters hut and stole inside to cover themselves in male attire. They arrived at the door flap of Saddam's tent, peeked inside to see the naked bodies of Saddam and Johanna mauling each other.

Saddam's clothes were draped across a chair by the bedside.

'It's now or never,' Niki whispered. She entered the tent while Melanie stood guard. Niki quietly crept to the chair. As she began to remove the keys from the belt clip, she saw Johanna look straight into her eyes. Johanna took hold of Saddam's face in both hands and delivered a passionate kiss to his mouth.

As Niki went to depart, some of the clothes fell from the chair. Saddam looked up. 'Hey!' he screamed, 'Give me that rifle quick.' Johanna grabbed a bayonetted rifle that stood by the other side of the bed. As Saddam was about to take it from her, she jabbed it forcefully into his gut several times. Saddam slumped to his death with an expression of utter surprise across his face.

'We're getting out of here,' Niki said.

'I'm coming with you,' Johanna responded as she hurriedly grabbed some robes. Johanna, Melanie and Niki ran to the Overlander, roared it into action and sped away.

Marlena, still in a bikini, came running after them. 'Wait for me,' she screamed. Marlena scrambled on board and they made their way to the main gate.

When the guards saw Johanna at the wheel, they were mystified and let the Overlander through.

A terrorist helicopter appeared ahead of the terrorist army. The crew spied the Legionnaires waiting in ambush. They began to drop grenades upon the ambushers. Ray took hold of a bazooka rocket gun and blasted the helicopter in mid-air.

The terrorist forces continued to advance to the onslaught of the Legionnaires. A bloody battle took place. Realizing the Legionnaires had the upper hand, Abdul Khayam gave the order to retreat. They began to flee back toward their headquarters. The Legionnaires were hot in pursuit.

The Overlander carrying the four women ran out of fuel and they parked it on the roadside. While they were wondering what to do, the retreating terrorist forces headed towards them. A terrorist truck pulled alongside. It had a front cabin that held three. Another three rode in the back under a tarpaulin cover.

The terrorists recognized the women and overpowered them at gun point, tied them up and manhandled them into the back of the truck.

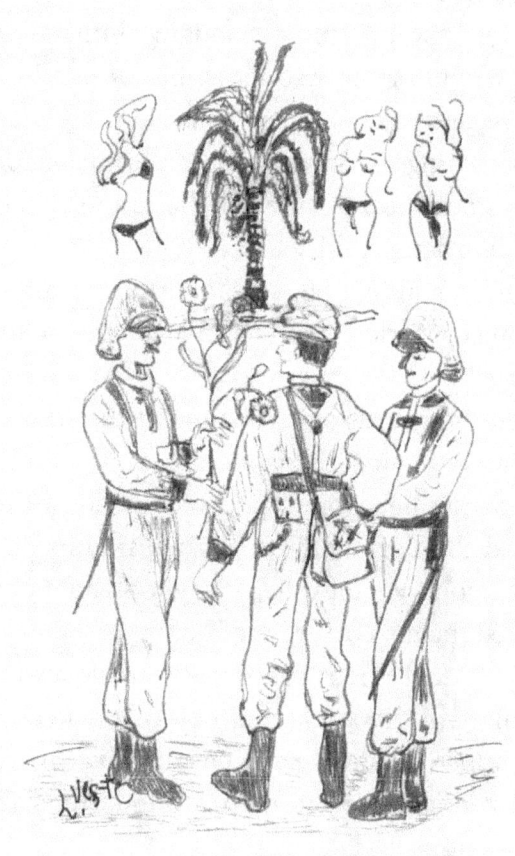

LILLIAN Tobescoff   Lillian

'Ahab Saddam will be most pleased with this little haul,' the driver said. Johanna smirked. Three terrorists got into the front, the others got into the back with the female captives.

The truck with Ray, Brian and Neville on board approached from further back. As they closed the gap, Brian looked ahead through binoculars. 'It looks mighty like some prisoners are being forced on board one of those trucks up ahead,' Brian said.' I'd say they could be women. One of 'em is for sure anyway. She's wearing a bikini.'

'Let's get up there and find out,' said Neville.

'I'll do my best,' Ray replied. 'I'll put this baby into full throttle.'

The truck with the women on board began to pull out to follow other retreating terrorist vehicles Ray turned his truck right across in front to block its path. The three Legionnaires disembarked, pistols in hand. A terrorist at the passenger window aimed a rifle at them. Brian swiftly pointed his pistol and fired. The bullet struck the rifleman right between the eyes. The truck door swung open and he fell to the ground.

'Nice work BJ,' said Neville.

The terrorist in the middle dived on to Brian. 'That was my brother you murdering scum,' he cried. He had a dagger in his hand ready to slit Brian's throat. Neville hit him on his head with his gun butt. The terrorist fell to the ground and reached for his dead brother's rifle. He abruptly stopped when Neville put a bullet into his chest.

In the meantime the driver got out of the other side, pistol in hand ready to shoot. He aimed at Neville but fell to the ground before he could fire due to a shot into his brain from Ray's pistol. Neville looked at Ray, gave a nod of gratitude. 'All for one and one for all,' said Ray.

Two of the remaining terrorists jumped out of the back of the truck with bayonetted rifles in hand. They came charging at the Legionnaires. Brian quickly fired two shots bringing them both to the ground. 'Well done BJ,' said Ray. Brian grinned proudly.

'Who needs us?' said Neville.

'Are there any more?' Brian asked.

'There's still one in here,' Johanna cried from inside the back of the truck. The three Legionnaires went to look into the back of the truck. The four women were there, tied at their hands and feet.

The last of the terrorists was crouching beside Melanie with his gun barrel jammed at the side of her face. 'Come one inch closer and she's dead meat,' he warned. 'Drop your guns.'

'Don't do anything stupid,' said Ray. 'You're in a 'no win' situation.'

'I'll take at least one with me,' the terrorist replied. 'Now you let me out of here with one of these dames as hostage and go on your merry way. Otherwise I will start by blasting this one's brains out.'

All in a flash, Johanna kicked her tied feet at the terrorist's hand, knocking his gun flying. Caught off guard, the terrorist flung himself onto Niki. He placed his hands around her throat and began to strangle her. Melanie positioned herself where she could place her mouth to one of his hands and savagely bit at it, drawing lots of blood.

Neville and Brian overpowered the terrorist while Ray used a knife to cut the tied up women free. The ropes were re-used to tie up the terrorist who was taken as a prisoner. The women were relieved when they realized they were rescued.

'We are so thankful and proud of you men for rescuing us. We're going to tell our Dad all about you when we get back home,' said Niki.

'He's a British Earl you know,' Melanie added.

'Mmm, I had a hunch he might have been,' Ray mused.

Fuel was syphoned into the Overlander, the terrorist's truck was taken over and the three trucks began their way back to Commander Jordan's Fort. Johanna rode with Neville. Marlena rode with Brian and the Bird sisters accompanied Ray on the journey.

Ray, Brian and Neville became known as 'The Three Legionnaires'. They shared many adventures together in the years that followed.

THIS STORY was inspired by Alexandre Dumas's classic tale, *The Three Musketeers*.

THE ORPHAN WALLABY

Vera Murray

MUM Ronsa, the rock wallaby, clung closer to the wall with baby Bozo snug in her pouch as the flood water whirled and pounded around the rocks below. Ronsa's eyes searched the route her husband Davey had taken when he left to locate long grass for their next meal. He had not returned.

Without warning, a whirlpool of fast moving water swung around and upwards, almost throwing them into the melee. As it withdrew, Ronsa quickly and desperately jumped across the closest rock and on to a higher ledge. This enabled her to scramble further up and on to the road above.

As Ronsa bounded along the road in fear, truck lights blinded her. She was flung off her feet as the vehicle brushed her aside. Pain overwhelmed her as she rolled over and over to lay unconscious, on a grassy verge. Baby Bozo, filled with fear, found he could no longer hold on inside his mother's pouch. He was flung out into the cold wet air. He instinctively extended his paws out in front of him to protect his face as he rolled into long grass. 'Mummy...mummy!' he cried as loud as he could, but there was no answer.

He tried to scramble back up the slope and on to the road to find his mother, but it rose too sharply. With a cry of dismay he felt he would never see her again. He frantically tried to climb, but his feet kept slipping on wet slimy mud, until his legs hung loose and his hands could no longer hold on. Bozo felt himself slide downwards. He tried to grab a tuft of tall grass but failed. As his body reached ground level he continued down a tunnel-like hole in the ground. He closed his tear-filled eyes until he stopped moving. He lay there in pain, trying not to cry. Hearing voices he opened his eyes to see the two occupants of the hole gather around him.

'Look, we have a little brother,' said the tiny voice of an infant meerkat.

'He's crying,' said the other as he looked into Bozo's face. 'Don't cry. You're shaking. You're cold. We'll keep you warm.' Immediately their warm bodies were pressed against him.

'What's your name? Mine's Gilly and this here with me is my sister Wandy. What's your name?'

'Bozo,' muttered the little rock wallaby as he took in a deep breath, 'and I'm an orphan now.'

As Gilly was about to ask what an orphan was, Wanda spoke. 'Look Gilly, what funny feet he's got, and, he's got funny biggish ears and nose, not like ours.' They both giggled.

A shadow blocked the entrance to the nursery. They turned to see their babysitter Boolie peering in. 'What's all the giggling about?' she asked.

'Our new little brother looks funny,' Gilly and Wandy answered in chorus.

Boolie entered the nursery and scratched the side of her neck with one of her paws in wonderment when she saw Bozo. 'I'm off having something to eat and look what happens. Tell me, where did this strange baby came from? It's deformed. Who put it in here when my back was turned?

Gilly and Wandy looked vague.

'Right! I'll find out, I will indeed.' She gave another quick glance at the babies before returning to her outside position of guard.

When the group returned that evening Boolie questioned every female to try to discover whose baby it was, but every one of them, wide-eyed with surprise, denied any knowledge of a deformed baby. Boolie decided she would wait and keep watch to see who in the group took extra interest in the baby's welfare. That one, she decided, would be the mother. Weeks went by and Boolie was no closer to getting an answer.

Meanwhile, Bozo grew bigger and taller than his meerkat 'siblings'. He began to go on trips with them, at which the elders showed them how to recognise signs of potential danger, and, as important, how to find food. Bozo astounded them by not digging for food but eating grass. 'He must be still sick and green stuff makes him feel better. He'll gradually discover that insects and the like are much better fare,' spoke up Boolie when questioned. On these daily runs Bozo kept looking around for any sign of creatures like himself, but he saw none.

One morning the camp was on alert. Alarmed voices told Bozo that those on lookout duty saw a group advancing towards them, and only the defence group would stay outside to protect them from a possible invasion. Bozo was ordered back inside one of the burrows so he would be safe. Curious, he waited until he knew the guards would be checking the other end of the settlement. He then peered out.

He heard 'thump thump' of heavy feet. There was something familiar about the sound, so he crept out, leapt across the narrow open area before him, and quickly hid behind a large tall clump of grass on the other side of their area.

There was something familiar about the sound, so he crept out, leapt across the narrow open area before him, and quickly hid behind a large tall clump of grass on the other side of their area.

As the sound of advancing footsteps grew close, Bozo, feeling more nervous, drew back, deeper into the scrub. The visitors were almost directly in front of his hiding place when he heard a voice say, 'He must be around here somewhere. He wasn't found near me.' Bozo sucked in his breath. It sounded like his mother's voice. Then another voice Bozo was convinced was his father's, spoke. 'Are you sure?'

'Yes. It was up on the road we just jumped down from, and where I showed you I was hit, and where that Good Samaritan found me, and, looked after me until I recovered.'

Now convinced they were his parents Bozo leaped out of his hiding place to flop down before them. 'Mother, Father,' he cried. Within seconds he was receiving a warm and weepy embrace from his parents. He briefly told them about the meerkats who adopted him. You must come and meet all my friends.'

His parents, eager to thank their son's saviours, walked with Bozo towards the meerkat guards. Seeing Bozo with his arms held away from his body they relaxed, and informed their leaders, who came forward. After a brief conversation they welcomed Bozo's parents.

After considerable discussion and exchanging of information, it was finally decided that the area they were in could be shared between the grass-eating wallabies and the meerkats, especially as Bozo would always be considered as a member of the meerkat family.

Boolie, watching on, sighed with content, for the mystery of the 'deformed baby' and its strange eating habits was solved.

INSPIRED BY the TV series that covered meerkats' lives in the wild.

RUMOURS

David MacLaughlin

BRISBANE International Airport at 11pm is anything but alive, Frank mused to himself. He had twenty minutes until boarding started on his flight to Hong Kong. The place was dead except for passengers awaiting outward flights. He had been on inward international flights and there was so much hustle and bustle with more passengers than the airport administration could handle. But these late night flights were a different story. No eateries open, but the duty free was. That was ok if you wanted a Rolex or Scotch whisky, for which he had no need.

Frank was part of a small group of intelligence officers who were going to an information exchange meeting with the Chinese from Beijing. He was different from his colleagues being Indigenous. His father was Aboriginal and his mother of Irish-Australian descent. He had been brought up in Cunnamulla and his dad taught him 'a love of country' and his mother encouraged his formal education.

He had studied law and he had a keen sense of adventure .In time, he ended up in an intelligence unit that checked out internet gossip and rumours that related to terrorist attacks on Australian citizens worldwide. Frank was thinking about the present chatter which fuelled rumours about a possible sabotage using chemicals which were to be released into a major Australian metropolitan area. His colleagues used 'white fella' research and logic when trying to decode 'chatter'. Frank understood that and how code breakers worked during the Second World War to crack German and Japanese coded military messages.

Yawning, Frank stroked his black hair and for relaxation recalled a dream time story of how the Bribie sand bar and Mount Coolum had come into existence. He quietly marvelled at how these myths explained geographical features in a poetic language.

There was gossip going around about the release of chemicals into a city reservoir. It would be fatal to anyone who drank the water from that supply. The poison was not detectable by any known water treatment and that was why the gossip had to be sourced.

Potentially it was not idle chatter but a rumour. If correct there was a possibility of a serious loss of life. He and the group had poured over countless internet messages, and the consensus was that a water reservoir would be targeted. The problem was where, and how to deal with it. 'Why are we going to Hong Kong when the event may happen right here in Queensland?' Frank muttered to himself. The Hong Kong trip was part of a joint meeting with other international agencies working for the world's democracies. Such meetings were usually good for problem solving.

But Frank was restless and felt like going on a mental 'walk about'. His white fella mates usually joked with him when he was mentally thinking about other things as he had that faraway look in his eyes. Frank, had a deep love of country as well as being patriotic about Gallipoli, and deep feelings for a land his ancestors had been on for 40,000 years. None of his colleagues could match that.

The Airbus took off .He was always amazed that it took five hours to finally leave behind the Australian island continent. The rest of the group talked idly. They had a few drinks in business class as the Airbus was traversing the continent. Frank chatted but he would often glance through the small window and wonder at the immense brown land below him. 'If I was wanting to create havoc outside a major city, where would I dump my poison?' The poison affected crops as well as humans, Frank had learned from previous briefings. He had accepted that, it sounded logical. That was the trouble, all this white fella logic which forgot about using your brain creatively. He looked out of the Airbus window 25,000 feet above sea level .He saw large water expanses of land and water below him.

The water was the legacy of the recent cyclone that had crossed over part of the continent and left a deluge of water in some areas, and rest was in a grip of a drought. He had the uneasy feeling that a sabotage was more likely in the south east or south west part of his home state Queensland. In the Dream Time, mountains and valleys and lakes resulted when spirit figures were chased and then transformed into raised land forms and deep valleys that became lakes. He smiled to himself. The Dream Time had a bit of adventure about it.

When man changed the environment it was usually bad news. Like Cubbie Station, that huge man-made cotton growing area fed by dams along 28 kilometres of the Culgoa River that flows into the Darling River and into the ocean. Trouble is, the Darling, downstream from the dams, does not flow well except when flood rains come down in torrents. Farmers along the Darling hold irrigation rights for crop growing. Food is the major resource needed for this century not minerals. Frank was sure the sabotage attempt would be aimed at agriculture facilities not city buildings. Even 9/11 affected only part of New York. Poisoned water reserves could devastate a whole country. He was going off the idea of a city catastrophe and let his colleagues know.

'You're mad mate,' they chorused. 'Your mind has gone walkabout, yet again. Anyway we need to use that computer model the Chinese have in Hong Kong. That will change your mind. Dumping a bit of poison in Cubbies you must be mad. Somerset Dam yes, that makes sense. The whole of Brisbane would be poisoned. Cubbie, don't be stupid mate.' However, the group knew Frank had a good track record in deciphering 'chatter' and foiling sabotage attempts. So the computer modelling in Hong Kong should indicate if Cubbies Station was a likely target for chemical poisoning downstream.

The approach to Hong Kong prior to landing was spectacular. The steep mountains and crowded skyscrapers seemed to close in on the aircraft as it lost altitude and landed on the long new airstrip. Frank always thought about his large empty southern continent contrasted dramatically with densely populated Asia.

Hong Kong Island spread out before them.

The Beijing Chinese intelligence officers had received a series of intercepted messages which pointed to an attack somewhere in the region. The Chinese were puzzled by certain aspects of the messages. The words 'darling' and 'cotton' were words that the Chinese thought had no relevance to the sabotage. Frank smiled and let his group know that the computer modelling confirmed his thoughts that Cubbie was the target to watch out for.

The Chinese had no wish for vast areas of Australian agricultural land to be chemically poisoned. Their government was encouraging agricultural partnerships which would ensure future supplies of food for the country's huge population. Frank and the Aussie intelligence group also knew that China had plenty of data on the ramifications of polluted and poisoned waterways in their own huge country. Beijing was always on a pollution alert whenever Frank had been there for meetings with his Chinese counterparts.

Just as the Chinese hosts were passing around cups of refreshing green tea, a pile of printed emails and a summary was put on the table. A code had been broken and it was now evident that Cubbie was the target. What was worse was that the date for the sabotage was to be as soon as possible. The Australian group and the Chinese hosts were turning greener than the green tea as the realisation set in that Australia was going to be hit by the biological equivalent of a tsunami. Once the huge Cubbie water reserves were chemically poisoned, the water systems in place could not stop the flow of water going through the whole Darling system and causing irreparable damage. It would be too late to stop the devastation, even if the water was held back from the irrigation channels and natural water courses that flowed down through the Darling River system. Frank was worried.

The group was nonplussed and the Chinese appreciated the devastation that could occur. The same thing could have affected their huge river tributaries systems. Maybe, it was time to accept the chatter threat had been confirmed and start about a Dream Time solution. Frank had that faraway look in his eyes.

The view from the Brisbane Plaza building took in the winding river and Mt Coot-tha in the background. Frank had returned early from Hong Kong so he could concentrate on locating where the chemicals might be stored. If the location was found, it was only matter of making sure the chemical storage facility was closed to access by anyone. 'If the chemicals could not be put on a plane, then Cubbie was safe. For the present anyway,' he mused to himself. Chinese intelligence sources might even be able to determine where the location could be.

But Frank had another way to locate the chemical loading facility. He had a cousin and extended family around the St George area where Cubbie was centred. Using his training as an intelligence officer, Frank thought the most likely option for a sabotage attempt on Cubbie would be from a base close to the target area. Why bother using a metropolitan runway at the risk of being detected? Frank was convinced it would be close to Cubbie where the chemicals were to be released into its huge water catchment area. Now it was time to call in favours from some of his tribal cousins.

The *Balonne Beacon* newspaper headlines read 'Local Terrorist Attack '. Frank scanned the article. It was wordy but did not describe where the attack would be. The reference to the source of the information was interesting. Not the usual 'trusted source' but 'information gathered from local communities'. Frank rang his cousin, a ranger who knew all the dirt tracks fire-fighters used on training exercises. The cousin remembered the Beacon reporter who had been asking about unusual activity in the region.

He told Frank about mining exploration teams that explored the bush. Usually they did not build any structures, just drilled holes. However, one lot did put up a well camouflaged hut for storing materials. His cousin thought it was strange. Why bother storing equipment far away from the bitumen roads which provided easy access. There was room for a helicopter to land, he noticed. Frank thanked him and asked him to keep in touch as he wanted to see this place.

Frank was on his way to St George by road. He drove a seconded old utility which had military-standard communications equipment, night sensors and spotlights, as if he was going kangaroo shooting as a bounty hunter. Dream Time legends were on Frank's mind as he drove along the highway. The spirits often acted swiftly to turn the tables on those who displeased them. So in turn Frank felt his strategy must be to make a preventive strike against those planning to dump chemicals in Cubbie.

That made more sense than trying to locate where the terrorist cell group might be operating from. He was relying on his cousin's connection to locate the storage site. If he was wrong then the dastardly deed would be done, and the job of stopping the chemicals spreading through the water systems would be well-nigh impossible. One thing he was sure of, he thought, grinning to himself, nobody will take any notice of a 'black fella' wandering around the bush in a beat up utility with a dozen cans of beer on board. He had not told any of his superiors he was there. If any of the saboteurs were around he might be in danger.

Later he was navigating his way through a patch of scrub and light timber .Dust was billowing up behind the utility. The sun was starting to set, and a few kangaroos darted ahead of the ute. Frank swerved to avoid them and came to a sudden stop at the base of tangled scrub. 'Bloody roos', he muttered, 'nearly wrecked my ute.' He got out to inspect the damage, and as he was looking at the front bull bar, a kangaroo took fright and raced for cover in the nearby scrub. Frank walked over to where the scrub had been disturbed by the kangaroo taking off rapidly. Looking down he noticed some wheel tracks that ended at the edge of the bush. He peered through the broken foliage and his heartbeat increased. In front of him was a hut surrounded by barbed wire. He cautiously made his way around the perimeter, and saw a car track that led to the camouflaged hut. Walking back to his ute, he watched a bush turkey scuttle past. He turned around, and looked into the bush and saw a grinning black face with bright piercing eyes staring at him. 'You're getting slow in your old age,' the face said and on closer inspection his cousin was the source of the face. 'I could have donged you with a nulla nulla and you wouldn't have known where it came from.' .Once Frank got over the shock, he laughed and gave his cousin a brotherly hug. His cousin had learnt from some of his Indigenous mates who worked for a gas pipeline contractor that the hut had been recently built. This was unusual in the area, as no gas pipe line was anywhere near Cubbie water reserves. Lots of travellers stayed at the old Commercial Hotel in St George, included the mining and gas exploration teams. Anything suspicious would be relayed back to him quickly. One of Frank's sisters worked in dining at the old pub and she knew all the gossip and idle chatter of the drinking patrons.

Frank went back to the Commercial and over a few drinks he observed who was staying there. He wandered from group to group between the hotel bars. In the city he would have been ignored but here he could chat to anyone. Most were miners or gas team workers on contract and a few local graziers complaining about the lack of rain, as usual. Feeling tired he went to his room and was soon asleep.

He woke up with a start to the ring tone of his mobile. Half asleep, he mumbled into it. It was his cousin sounding excited, 'Get to the hut we saw earlier. My sister overheard a convo between a couple of so called gas fitters about getting spare parts for a plant near Cubbie. I'll meet you there'. Frank was soon on his way.

The ute had spotlights for 'roo shooting which could be handy if the suspects made a getaway from the hut. The ute raced along the bitumen and turned off where the dirt track began. Wheels were spinning and dust was billowing up behind him as he drove towards the hut in the bush. His plan was to drive the ute into the hut. This would prevent anybody taking the chemicals away. He turned a sharp right and the hut came in view. Frank slowed down to change into a lower gear. He need not have bothered. As he turned the ute front end dropped into a hidden ditch and came to a sudden stop. The saboteurs heard the loud thump.

They had already loaded up the chemical containers in their vehicle and raced off back down the track. Suddenly there was a loud whirring noise and a blaze of light. A helicopter appeared and shone its spotlights onto the fleeing ute and followed it down the track. The ute did not get far .Three utes appeared from nowhere and blocked it from going any further. The deadly plot was foiled.

Later Frank found out that his cousin and his mates knew more about the attempt on Cubbie than he did. The Forestry Department they worked for had been asked by the Intelligence Group for their cooperation in finding where the attempt on Cubbie would originate. They did not arouse suspicion as Aboriginals were often seen working for the exploration teams.

His cousin smiled at Frank after the successful event. Over a couple of cold ones he remarked, 'You're a smart cookie with all your degrees but us local blackfellas know more about what is going on around here.' Frank had been wondering what his intelligence unit had been doing while he was chasing around the bush. Now he knew they had been tracking his movements and using the talents of his own people to help track down where the saboteurs might be and where the chemicals were held.

The security media releases were frequently doctored to show how effective the unit was in protecting Australia's national interest. But this time a local reporter had heard some gossip in the pub. He heard of exploration teams operating outside normal business hours and how Frank has been protected by local Indigenous people. Instinctively he knew he had a scoop and feverishly completed his story before any official press release. The morning paper announced boldly to the Australian public, "Local Aboriginals foil terrorist attack on Cubbie'.

Needless to say, the National Security Agency was not impressed because it did not get all the credit for foiling the attempt. Frank grinned, he did not mind. He remembered that in World War 1, his Indigenous ancestors enlisted as volunteers to serve King and Country but were not classed as Australian citizens. They could die for Australia but could not vote. Times were changing and this time for the better. He headed to his cousin's place to catch up on family and go fishing for a week, before heading back to Canberra and more challenges.

INSPIRED BY a novel by Trish Sheppard, 1976's *Children of Blindness*, a controversial writing about life in an Australian country town. The main characters included local Aboriginal people.

KASPER BEAUMONT
& KYLA MILNE

SIENNA
The Huntress

The Beginning

Sienna the Huntress: the beginning
Kasper Beaumont and Kyla Milne

'HOORAY! I found a bee hive.' Fairy Sienna-Li was delighted to hear the buzzing high in a tree. He looked up and saw bees flying in and out of a hollow.

Halfling Sienna looked up and taunted him with a twinkle in her eyes, 'So, what are you waiting for, little pig; are you scared?' The fairy's face reddened in embarrassment as he flew up to inspect the hive, while chuckling Sienna climbed so their bond limit would allow him to reach the top.

A flapping sounded a split-second before a raven swooped down and grabbed the fairy who called in desperation, 'Help, help!'

Sienna jumped down and chased the bird through the woods as fast as she could run. 'Sienna-Li, noooooo.' Her chest heaved with exertion; her voice came out in ragged gasps. 'Let him go!' Tears welled in her eyes and she brushed them away.

The poor fairy's face was ashen. He trembled from head to toe; almost fainting from the fright. This caused Sienna to stagger as well.

The raven flew directly upwards and Sienna felt a sharp pain all over her body as the bond with her fairy neared its breaking point, which would kill them both.

Just when all seemed lost, the neighs of a herd of flying horses passing overhead distracted the raven, which flew back down to the trees.

The raven crowed an evil laugh and landed on a high branch still clutching its prey. A flock of ravens decided to join in the meal and surrounded him like a black cloud of death. Sienna glimpsed the fairy's terrified face all but blocked by the mass of birds.

The raven raked a claw along Sienna-Li's tiny arm and he screamed with pain as it bled.

Sienna gasped and grabbed her arm too as an angry red welt appeared, identical to that of her bond-fairy.

The halfling struggled to be brave and forced the pain and fear to the back of her mind. Her face tightened into a scowl, she felt her cheeks heat up, flamed with anger and indignation. Her hands blanched as she curled them tight into fists. She spoke through clenched teeth at the raven, 'Never take my fairy away from me.' Her heart pounded in her chest as she reached over her back and grabbed her father's spare bow and an arrow. Fumbling with uncertainty for she had never used a bow before, her trembling hands managed to notch the arrow which she aimed at the mass of birds. The first arrow flew off to the side with a harmless bounce off a tree. The halfling screamed in frustration.

Ignoring the sweat dripping from her palms, she wiped them on her trousers. She gritted her teeth, and with fingers trembling, again reset her bow. Sienna knew it would only be mere seconds before her fairy was killed, and thus she also, the bond's only weakness. The second arrow struck true and hit the raven square in the chest. It plummeted to the ground, dead.

As one, the remaining birds squawked in fright and sought the safety of the trees.

The body of Sienna-Li floated down like a leaf. The bow dropped to the ground as Sienna caught him with gentle hands.

'Sienna-Li, are you okay?' Tears rained down her cheeks and splashed onto the groaning fairy. She smoothed his hair with one finger and was relieved when he let out a big sigh.

His eyes shone on her with tenderness. 'My Sienna.' His voice was a thin whisper. 'You were so brave to save me.'

The fairy shivered and Sienna wrapped him in the corner of her old brown cloak. 'I used Father's bow to shoot the raven that captured you. I was terrified they might kill you instead.'

Fresh tears rained down on the fairy and he glowed from within as he brushed a tear from his face. 'I am sorry I demanded we go to the beehive. I should have listened to you and stayed near the cabin. Can we please go home now, dear one?'

'Of course. Let us leave this place.' Picking up the bow in one hand, she cradled her tired fairy and felt his weariness wash over her as well. The excitement of looking for honey had vanished in the tense skirmish and she began the long walk home.

'I never should have disobeyed Father. I nearly got you killed,' Sienna said. A tear slid down her face and the fairy caught it as it dropped off her chin.

Sienna remembered that morning when her father Harlon had ruffled her tangled brown hair, his weathered fingers catching on the knots. 'Tsk, tsk, you could use a good brush, Tangles.' Affection was clear in his voice and twinkling brown eyes. 'I'll get you a hairbrush on my trip to Greendale. Now, are you sure you'll be alright, here in the Wild Woods, all alone?'

'She's never alone, because she's with me!' Sienna-Li flapped his iridescent wings in front of Harlon's face. The fairy struck a protective pose as he returned to Sienna's shoulder. He was her constant companion due to their lifelong bond and always kept an eye on the young halfling. 'I'll make sure we stay safe and sound while you're away.' Harlon's fairy nodded her tiny head in agreement.

Harlon had gathered the reins of his pony, Patch, then hugged Sienna tight before he left. 'I know you two will be fine for your first time alone at home. Just beware the bears and wolves, and don't stray far from the cabin.' He drew up his grey hood and blew her a kiss. A gentle smile adorned his face as he watched his daughter trying to look brave as she waved.

Harlon-La nodded her belled cap in agreement as they set off down the road. The halfling whistled a tune and his fairy waved goodbye as she followed the plodding pony along the grassy path through the woods.

When they had gone from sight, Sienna-Li smiled at Sienna with cheeky dimples, 'Do you want some honey?'

Sienna stared at him with wide eyes, 'Already! You just had breakfast. You're a little pig, plus we are not leaving this cabin in search of a bee hive.'

Sienna-Li flew backwards and looked around. They were silent for a moment, until Sienna rolled her eyes. He tried again, 'Do we have any honey in the cabin?'

With a groan Sienna grabbed her father's spare bow and arrows and set off into the forest. 'C'mon, let's go.'

A grin of victory lit Sienna-Li's face and he chased after the brown halfling.

___oOo___

THE HALFLING and her fairy were on their long walk back to the cabin when they froze in their tracks.

Sienna looked wide-eyed at the dark shadows of the Wild Woods with the sounds of unseen animal noises scurrying through the underbrush. She hesitated.

The sound of a horse screaming caused goosebumps to break out on her arms. She ran towards the noise and saw to her surprise a young winged horse with long shaggy hair.

Sienna-Li leapt out of Sienna's arms, tested his iridescent wings briefly and flew to inspect the foal. 'Oh no, he has a broken wing.'

'It could be a she.' The halfling tried to sound knowledgeable.

'I spoke to his mind, it's a he.' The fairy snapped at her with irritation and turned back to the snowy-haired animal. He ran a glowing hand along the wing which hung down from the foal's shoulder. 'My powers won't be enough to heal this one. What are we to do with him?'

'Let's take him back to the cabin and see what we can find in Mother's old healing book.' Sienna approached the animal, which backed away warily. 'Come, foal. I'm here to help you.' Her voice was soft to offer him comfort.

The animal continued to shy away and reared up in alarm when Sienna approached him again. Her smile drooped in disappointment and she stepped backwards, wondering what she could do.

A chorus of neighs resounded from the sky, half-hidden through the trees.

'That must his herd.' Sienna-Li flew a little higher to see the winged horses. Large mounts of varying hues circled the area where the foal had fallen. 'I'd say this is his family, Sienna.'

One of the largest animals flew lower to greet the fairy and nudged him with a dry nose. The fairy glowed with pleasure and flew to the side, where he patted the grey-blue stallion's mane. 'His father here wants us to help his foal. He flew too low and crashed into a tree. The adults can't get down through the entwined branches, nor can they do anything to help mend his broken wing.'

'OK, let's try and walk him home to our cabin.' Sienna approached the foal again and this time, he trembled and allowed her to stroke his face. With a gentle touch, the halfling guided him through the Wild Woods back to the cottage and the foal followed in silence. The halfling failed to notice that small pools of water welled up from the ground each time the pony stepped.

Sienna-Li lit the way with his fairy glow. 'Can we call him Sparkles?'

Sienna frowned. 'That's what everyone calls them. How about Magic?'

'That's a bit better. How about Misty? He's the colour of mist.' The fairy's bell tinkled as he nodded his head with enthusiasm.

'Perfect.' They both smiled and slapped hands in a high-five.

They continued their happy banter as they approached the cabin.

'You wait out here Sienna-Li and I'll go and find the healing book. It's such a shame Mother died when I was born; Father said she was the best healer in the South Lands.' After a quick rummage around, she returned with the book opened at a page for making a poultice. 'I'm not very good at reading the names of ingredients, but we can look at the pictures and figure it out.'

'I've seen some of those roots in the kitchen and there are some of those ruffled leaves growing behind the cabin.' Fairy and the halfling gathered the ingredients as fast as they could and mixed them in a pot with a little water. Sienna spread the mixture over the break in Misty's wing. The foal shuddered, but allowed them to complete the task and bandage a straight branch along the wing to make a splint.

Sienna was so deep in concentration that she jumped with surprise when the stallion nudged her from behind and gave a low nicker. She spun around to see the entire family of winged horses had crept up to be near their injured foal. Each came forward and nudged her hands in gratitude.

'You're welcome.' Her big brown eyes blinked back tears of emotion and she smiled at the gentle animals.

'Look at the water springing from the ground where they stand.' Sienna-Li flew around and around in excitement, marvelling at the magic.

The dull thud of hooves on the track caused the winged horses to draw back into the shadows of the trees. Sienna spied Harlon's grey coat, then his pony. 'Papa!'

As she ran towards him, he bounded down from his mount and spun Sienna around. 'How did you go all alone in the woods, my brave daughter?

Her words came forth in a babble of excitement. 'Sienna-Li was captured and I shot a raven with your bow, and we helped the winged horses and I made a poultice . . . .'

'Whoa, little one. You certainly have had a very busy day. It sounds like you take after both your parents, an ability with the bow and an affinity with healing like your late mother.' He looked into her shining brown eyes and saw bravery which had not been there before. He stroked her tangled hair with pride. 'Can you take off that tattered old cloak? I have a present for you.'

The cape dropped to the ground. He pulled a package from his satchel. 'This is such an appropriate occasion for this gift. It is the cloak of a huntress, so from now on we shall call you 'Sienna the Huntress.' I'm so proud of you using my bow and helping this wounded animal.' He wrapped a new green cloak around his daughter and pulled the green hood onto her head. Sienna beamed with pride.

The winged foal walked up to Harlon and his winged herd all gathered around them, neighing with pleasure.

INSPIRED BY the writings about hobbits by J.R.R. Tolkien

SOMEONE TO WATCH OVER ME

Bernie Dowling

January 1, 1991, 3pm, Hendra, a Brisbane suburb

SEVEN, SIX, FIVE...I opened my eyes to see what the countdown was about.

'Happy New Year!' It came from the television set.

'Where am I?' I muttered.

Wearing only boxer shorts, I was lying prone. I put my chin in my palm with my elbow on the collapsible couch. 'What's this?' I asked myself about the couch, which the Brits call a sofa, and we call a lounge in Australia. It is not to be confused with the television, coffee-imbibing and reading room which we also call a lounge.

'Happy New Year, Steele Hill.' This time it came from a young woman with long black hair, sitting on the lounge in front of me. She wore only a black bra and matching panties.

I kissed her on the shoulder and replied, 'Happy New Year, Natalie Applebee.' I pushed Nat's right bra strap gently down her shoulder. 'Hangover sex,' I said romantically. I meant it to be romantic but, croaked from a mouth rancid with stale alcohol, it might have fallen short of my intention.

Natalie replaced the strap and turned around, showing her beautiful, though blurry-eyed, face. Nat had turned 21 in 1990, a big occasion on anyone's calendar. 'We did that two hours ago,' she said.

'With each other?' I asked. I had turned 25 in 1990. I don't think mid-decade birthdays count for much.

'That's insulting,' she said. 'But I'm sure you will tell your gambling mates down the pub how great it was.'

'I always do, Nat,' I said. 'Out of respect for you.'

It is a variation of a routine My Cucumber and I have going, based on old joke. Q. Why do Australian men having sex come so quickly? A.

176

So they can rush down to the pub to tell their mates about it. I inhaled the lingering aroma of recent sex in case that needed to sustain me for the rest of the day. Natalie might be up for some more hangover sex, you know, for auld lang syne. 'Go brush your teeth, now,' she said, but the way it came out did not sound like a promise. 'It's 3pm,' she added. The significance of the time eluded me until she explained, 'Normal people have been up for hours, even on New Year's Day.'

When I got back, Natalie had donned a T-Shirt from a tour of an English band, the techno/guitar hybrid Pop Will Eat Itself. No encore sex seemed likely but you never know you luck in the big city. My best mate, 60-year-old illegal bookmaker Con 'Gooroo' Vitalis, says Australian humourist Lenny Lower coined the phrase 'you never know your luck in the big city'. Good one Len, there are worse philosophical foundations to build a life on.

I sat beside Nat and put my hand around her waist, fairly high up but below her breast. I needed to show I was not a cad in case an opportunity arose later. 'Whatcha watchin'?' I asked.

'It's New Year's Eve live in Times Square in New York. A big ball is coming down from the sky.'

I could see it. This gigantic balloon festooned with red white and blue lighting was sliding down this huge metal pole. Watching my modest TV, I could not tell whether the ball was perched on the pole like a huge lollipop and the metal stick was retracting. Or the ball was sliding down the pole like a fireman on a mission to save New York and, by extension, the free world. Buddha, it was impressive, but.

The lights on the ball went out and it disappeared behind a gigantic sign which said 1991. Wow! The 300,000 people in the square began hoopin' and hollerin'.

The CBS network grabbed us by the eyeballs to rush us across to the Waldorf-Astoria Hotel ballroom where balloons rained down on the well-heeled revellers. Most of the balloons looked to be computer generated by the good techies at CBS. So much more reliable to pop on cue.

An instant later, we are at Billy Bob's Texas, a country-music barn in Ft. Worth. From the stage the talent is singing *Auld Lang Syne* and the punters are joining in, waving balloons, hugging and kissing. I had read somewhere President George Bush's daughter-in-law Laura was a Texan but I could not see her in crowd. I gotta stop reading all this shit which makes me search for Laura Bush when I do not know what she looks like.

'Wow,' I heard Natalie say. She turned her head towards me. 'These television crews have gotta be on speed.' Speed is methamphetamine in Australia. I believe it is also crack cocaine in the US.

'I bet those bathrooms got a real workout from coke snorters at 11.55,' I said.

'Speaking of coke, you got any soft drink in the fridge, Steele. All this excess is making me thirsty.' Soft drink is soda pop and I returned to the couch with two small plastic bottles of spring water.

When I sat beside Natalie, Billy Bob's had calmed down. On the screen a bearded country singer, dressed all in black, was about to perform. A subtitle told us he was Eddie Rabbit and he broke in to a ditty called *American Boy*. It did not do much for me and I noticed Nat ungraciously curl her top lip. The punters at Billy Bob's were enraptured. Some sang along; others wiped away tears. I guess you had to be there.

'Is there anything else on?' I asked.

'You're not watching the horse racing.'

'It's Tuesday, Nat; there's none on.'

I could have subscribed to the Sky satellite racing which broadcast daily but it cost an arm and a leg. Apart from the pubs and clubs, only the biggest professional punters hired it. My illegal bookie mate, the Gooroo, did not have it. He made do with the radio and said Sky was too distracting. He did not say, but we both knew, Sky and the PubTABs where you watched it were fast wiping out his industry.

Nat's demand that I desist from horse racing reminded me I needed to duck down later to the local PubTAB for a punt. I had not studied any form but I have a theory winning on New Year's Day is a good omen for the twelve months ahead. Gall it my variation on a new-year resolution. Call it ridiculous superstition. I don't really care.

It looked like we were persisting with this channel as CBS twinkled us back to the Waldorf-Astoria. The announcer warned us not to go away as the cast of the Broadway musical *Okay* was coming across from the theatre.

'They called a musical *Okay*, I said. 'Americans really are an optimistic lot, in their popular entertainment, at least.'

Natalie did her haughty voice to spell it out for me. 'It's O-H-, K-A-Y-! *Oh, Kay!* Nat even spelled out the capital-O, the comma, Capital-K and exclamation mark. I do appreciate Nat's character flaw of condescension. Without it, she might have hauled in a better romantic catch than me, if that is possible. Once Nat starts delivering a lesson it is rarely pithy.

'It's a revival of the 1926 George and Ira Gershwin musical.'

Sometimes I can throw Natalie off-tack with an irrelevancy. '1926, that's heaps older than any of my film-noir videos. I'm feeling thoroughly modern, culturally.'

No go, this time. 'It's where that Ella Fitzgerald song comes from, *Someone to Watch over Me.*'

'Don't know it.'

'Of course you do; I play it all the time.'

'Is it kind of soppy? I prefer her tough stuff like *Strange Fruit.*'

'Forget it, Steele. You have the sensitivity of a dried pea.'

'Sensitivity of a dried pea,' I repeated. 'That's clever, Nat, but it is somewhat inappropriate when we are canoodling on my new lounge.'

Nat involuntarily laughed. Nat loves words and I knew I would get to her with a crazy one like canoodling. She nudged the lounge with an open palm. 'Where did you get this? Something just doesn't seem right about it. The colour is awlright.'

A muted yellow fabric covered the lounge or sofa or couch, whatever you like to call it. The neutral colour was not the problem. I had discovered what the problem was soon after the Gooroo and I dragged it in. I have a tiny one-bedroom flat, all I can afford.

'It's too big,' I said to Nat. 'It has just arrived and it's taken over the place.'

'Didn't you think of that before you bought it?'

'Gooroo gave it to me; said it was from one of his flats they were sprucing up.'

Natalie had met the Gooroo a few times. They got on well without knowing much about each other. 'Gooroo's a landlord?' she asked.

I had thought little about it. 'Guess so,' I said. 'I never grill people about their dark side.'

Natalie laughed ruefully. 'How are you ever going to have money, Steele, when you think people who make a fair bit of it are monsters?'

'Gooroo is not a monster. His core business is honest.'

'I see. Gooroo's illegal gambling business is honest and his legal property investment is dishonest.'

'That's the way I see it. I'm not asking anyone to agree with me.'

The conversation was making me uneasy and I was glad that performers were on stage at the Waldorf. It was not the cast of *Oh, Kay!*

Kid Creole and the Coconuts, a Latin style band, was strutting its stuff with the number *Caroline*. Kid Creole seemed to be a Black guy in a Cab-Calloway style groove tuxedo and tails as well as a Russian style round fur hat with obviously artificial hair extensions protruding from beneath it. The band had guitars, percussion, piano and a horn section. Two White women danced on stage to the audience's left and another White woman gyrated less expansively on the right. It looked pretty weird, which was all right by me.

But the song failed to engage Nat and me so we talked over the top of it.

'Didn't they do that Prince song which they play on the radio sometimes?' I asked.

Nat is a huge Prince fan. For me, he is a pleasant enough way to pass the time. His albums and videos scream to me *kid with too much pocket money.*

Natalie recalled the name of the Prince song *The Sex of It.* 'Maybe they thought some of the audience might be offended,' she said.

The camera panned the crowd. 'Most of this lot are talking among themselves; they are not even listening,' I said.

Nat and I shared an annoyance about rock punters at live gigs who sat or stood up the front and talked while a band performed. How rude and how it must piss off bands, many of which are playing for peanuts. At least Kid Creole and the Coconuts could not see or hear Natalie and me talking over their song.

'Who are the Coconuts?' I asked.

'I believe they are the White women dancing and doing back-up vocals.'

'Wow, is that really wrong or totally cool?'

'I don't know,' Natalie admitted.

We had New Zealand Maori friends who lampooned Coconuts who were uncomfortable in their dark skins. Brown on the outside white on the inside, Coconuts; geddit?

'I think he actually did a song called *Don't Take my Coconuts,*' Natalie said.

'That guy's out there. They shoulda had him at Billy Bob's. That would have been fun.'

'Whoa, Dude, what are you doing here?' Nat did not say it. I did not say it. The TV did not say it. A man about 20 said it.

He was standing at the edge of my lounge, that is the room, not the couch. He had longish straggly sandy hair and matching stubble on his chin. His T-shirt told of a tour by the three-chord band, The Hard-Ons, who had an eclectic following of surfers, skaties, hardcores and people like me. He wore long shorts, if you know what I mean, and low-cut sports shoes which would have cost five times as much as the rest of his apparel combined.

I instinctively stood up and walked in front of Nat. The man clutched at the bottom of his shorts and a wooden knob appeared above his T-shirt. He extracted a baseball bat with his left hand and held it in his right. 'Don't come near me, dude,' he said as he did this punk-dance, kinda lightweight David Thomas of Pere Ubu, if you know what I mean. If you don't you had better look it up if you want the full picture. The bloke's hand holding the bat was shaking even more than the rest of him.

'Where's you red ute?' he said. 'It's not outside.'

'We left it at Bub's share house before we went out last night. We got a cab home.' I realised he would not know Bub was Nat's sister Jane but why was I telling this stuff, anyway?

'When I saw the ute was not there, I thought you weren't home. I have one just like it.'

'You came here to steal my car.' I walked towards him; I swear I don't know why.

He swung the bat in my direction and I took the blow on my extended right palm. 'Oww,' I said. 'Oww.'

'Hey,' Nat had stepped out from behind me and the man turned in her direction. She kicked him full in the nuts with her right foot. I winced as he crumbled to the floor and I said 'oww', but more quietly.

Natalie rushed over to grab the bat which the bloke had dropped. He curled up on the floor and both his hands protected his genitals. It was a bit late for that, now.

'I saw that,' Natalie said to me.

'Saw what.'

'Saw you cringe when I kicked him in the balls. Honestly, you men.'

'No I didn't,' I said. 'It was the pain. I think he broke my hand. And even if I did, that's empathy. That's good, right?'

'I'll give you empathy,' she said. Luckily, she turned on our invader. 'As for you, you make a move and I'll squash your skull like a watermelon.' She waved the bat around like Joe di Maggio who is the only baseball player I know apart from Babe Ruth but Simon and Garfunkel never put the Babe in a song.

'Show me your hand,' Nat said. Her eyes darted between my palm, with a red welt across it, and our unwanted guest.

'The only bones likely to be broken are in your thumb and below the finger next to it,' Nat said. 'Move that finger.'

I moved the finger. 'Oww.'

'That looks awlright. Move your thumb.'

I moved my thumb. 'Oww.' Maybe it didn't hurt as much as I first thought.

'Sorry, dude.' The man had recovered and was sitting on the floor.

'Shut fucking up, you,' My Cucumber said. Unlike most of our friends, Nat rarely swore, the exceptions invariably directed at me. Nat said swearing was an abuse of the English language. But now she was pumped as she gripped the bat. One clenched hand below the other swung it back and forth. I doubted she was capable of crunching our guest's skull but his expression showed she was fooling him big time.

'That's a pretty impressive stance you got there, Slugger,' I said. Did you play softball in high school?'

'I sure did, team captain, only it was in primary school, and the game was called rounders.'

'You never told me that.'

'Yair sure, that was going to come up. Hot fucking rock band, Steele, reminds me of when I used to play rounders in primary school.'

I reckon some band should do a song about playing rounders. Angie Hart from Frente! would be perfect for the vocals. I logged that in my memory to drop into a conversation with Nat. Now was not the time.

'Call the police, Steele!'

'We don't wanna do that. He'll do a bolt. You'll squash his head like a watermelon. I'll get blood all over the linoleum. The cops'll ask me why I keep the front door unlocked. The whole thing'll be a mess.'

'Why do you keep your door unlocked?' Nat asked.

'You do, too.'

'Yair, but not all the fuckin' time.'

'I've never been robbed.'

'Yair, I'm Steele Hill and I never robbed anyone so I've got good karma and I leave my front door open.'

'I don't say it like that.'

'I've robbed you before.' It was the voice from the floor.'

'Have not.'

Natalie smiled nastily at me. 'Do tell, Mr Robber. It might save you a night in the police watch-house.'

The man appeared to ignore Natalie's remark and he looked at me. 'Dude, how do you think I know about your red ute and that you keep your door open?'

'I don't keep it open. I leave it unlocked. And if you thought no one was home, why did you bring a baseball bat.'

'Precaution.'

'Yair, well, break and enter with a concealed weapon is serious jail time.

'I did not break in. The door was...'

'Let's not keep going over old ground.'

Natalie, on the other hand, liked old ground. 'No, go on, what'sya name.'

'Lance. I don't want to start a fight between you too. I should just go. Give me back me bat and I'll go.

Nat waved the bat around some more to show that was not going to happen.

I looked down on the man. 'Well, you did not get anything of value because I would have known so it was a waste of time.'

'I found two $50-notes in a book.'

I jigged a bit on my feet. 'You're lying, Lance.'

'The book was called *The Crucible* and it was in the bottom drawer in the kitchen under a pile of newspaper stories about a crooked horse race in 1986. That was why I left the TV and stereo. I figured I would get them next time.'

'Ha,' said Natalie. 'Is this the next time or have you accepted Steele's open invitation on other occasions?'

Lance put a hand to the floor to push himself erect. Natalie menaced him with her little friend and Lance stayed on the floor to explain. 'A little while after I found the fifties, I was doing furniture removals down this street. That was when I saw Steele drive away in his red ute and I remembered I was supposed to come back here.'

'When you say furniture removal...?' I asked.

'Not stealing them. I was an offsider for a furniture removalist.'

'You should have stuck with that job, mate.'

'The boss said work had dried up and he would give me a call. He never did.'

Natalie looked at both of us and unleashed her sarcastic voice. 'If you boys are finished reliving old crimes, what are we going to do with him, Steele?'

I thought about it. 'Where's your car?' I asked our guest.

'Parked outside.'

'That's pretty careless.'

'I stole the number plates.'

'So you have stolen number plates. How's your registration?'

'It's up to date. The cops can't get me there.'

'Stolen number plates which every traffic cop in Queensland would have the details of but a rego sticker which tells those same cops who you are and where you live?'

'Never thought of that.'

'The entrance exam for a career of crime has a zero failure rate. Here is what we are doing.' My stern face turned to Natalie. 'I am putting on my pants. Lance and I are signing a good behaviour bond. Nat, like in the movies, you watch him.'

I went to my bedroom and returned in T-shirt and jeans to find the situation as before.

'Good,' I said. 'Lance, you will promise not to come back to my place, ever. You will also promise to give up break and enters. Of course, I will not know if you fail that part of the agreement unless you come back here. To seal our deal, I am giving you this collapsible lounge.'

Natalie's scrunched up her face but it soon became placid. 'That's not a bad plan and I'll break Lance's wrist to seal my part of the deal.'

'What if you just break his wrist if he comes back?'

'Awlright,' Natalie said.'

'Come on, Lance, help me with the lounge.'

'Hang on; you'll just call the cops when I drive away.'

'Definitely not. They might bring you back here and that would be a breach of our agreement. By the way, throw me your car keys.'

'What?'

'We can't have you driving off without the lounge. Why are you so suspicious, Lance? You're the one who is a crim while Nat and I are honest law-abiding citizens.'

'Well, I am,' Natalie said.

I pouted in her direction and she laughed. This is why I love My Cucumber.

We put the lounge on the tray of Lance's ute but I was concerned. 'I don't know if it will stay there.'

In answer, Lance fetched four long strong dark-green straps from the cab.

He strapped the lounge to side bars of the ute, which turned out to be an old blue Falcon, nothing like my red Holden. Lance was a sloppy thinker.

I turned my thoughts to the plastic binds. 'You stole those straps from your employer, didn't you, Lance?'

'They call them ties,' he said.

'The same employer who told you work had dried up.'

Lance stopped tying for a couple of seconds, stood up, shrugged and resumed his task.

I could see Natalie watching us from the kitchen window. She had put aside her little friend. 'I suppose you are on parole,' I said to Lance.

'Probation.'

'That's just as bad. When you get caught next, they will bang you up for your previous crime, as well.'

He stood up. 'That's not right. That would be, whadatheycallit, double jeopardy.'

'It is not double jeopardy; you were found guilty the first time and punishment was deferred subject to your good behaviour. Didn't you listen to your duty solicitor?'

'Not really, I don't think she liked me.'

'She's not paid to like you. She's paid to keep you out of jail.'

'I've got her phone number. I'll ask her to explain it again.'

'Good idea. Speaking of phone numbers, give me yours. You look pretty handy with those ties. I have a mate down Tweed Heads. He knows lots of people; one of them might have some work for you.'

Having finished his tying, Lance stood to full height. 'Thanks,' he said. 'You are a very strange dude, Steele. I don't get you at all.'

'I like to keep them guessing.'

'Maybe we could have a beer or a bong some time.'

'Sorry, that would break our agreement. Maybe I'll run into you in a couple of years.'

'Sure. Say goodbye to Natalie. I really thought she was gunna do me some serious harm.'

'Me too,' I lied. 'You better ditch those stolen plates when you get home.'

He nodded, hopped into the ute and drove away. For some reason, I waved goodbye.

Inside my flat, I felt Natalie pinch me lightly. 'That was very nice, Steele. Stupid and futile, but nice.'

'It's your fault anyway, Nat. I can't get out of my head the theory you told me that one person's actions can change the life of someone, otherwise destined to be a loser.'

'I think it is more than a theory; it is a reality, but I doubt Lance will be adding to the positive results.'

'You never know your luck in the big city,' I said. 'Hey look, the new-year program is still on.'

Natalie and I placed my two armchairs beside each other in front of the TV and we made ourselves comfortable. President George H. W. Bush came on and he was beside a fireplace with real logs burning or maybe fake logs with electrical elements.

'He's up late,' I said, before a caption made a liar of me by saying the segment was recorded earlier.

'Happy New Year, America,' President Bush began.

'Welcome to another year where the new wind of freedom is blowing across the world.'

'Is that the same wind as Bob Dylan's answer is blowin' in?' I asked the TV.

'Shush,' said Natalie. 'I wanna hear what he has to say.'

'When you good people of America, you great people of America, elected me President, I promised that together we would see the passing of the totalitarian era.'

He looked at a sheet of paper in his hand. I guess he did not trust a teleprompter. 'I said at the time, 'The totalitarian era is passing, its old ideas blown away like leaves from an ancient, lifeless tree.'

'And it is. It may not seem so as one of the last dictators, Saddam Hussein, has seen fit to invade his neighbour Kuwait. But the era of the dictator is passing.

'Saddam Hussein, the last dictator, threatened another neighbour Saudi Arabia this year or, I should say, last year. The Saudi Government requested our help, and I responded to that request in August by ordering US air and ground forces to deploy to the Kingdom of Saudi Arabia.

'I won't stand by to watch a friend in trouble.

'I asked the CBS crew taping this address what other coverage they had because I might like to watch it or have someone tape it for me.

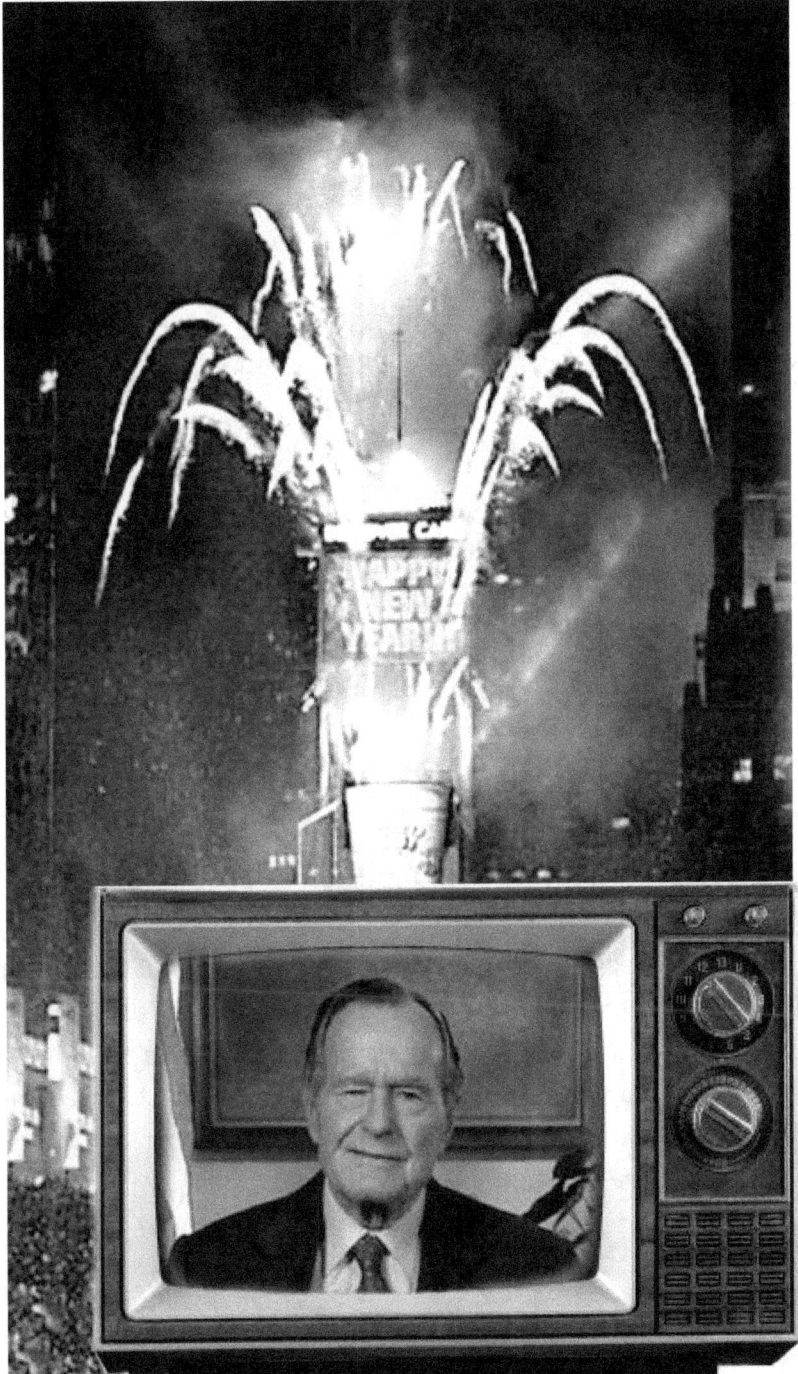

They told me they were taking music from Billy Bob's in Ft. Worth. Some of you might not know this but I was the first Republican in history to represent Houston in our Federal House.

'So I know Billy Bob's in Ft Worth which is a morning jog away from Houston, about 250 miles, from memory. I have been to Billy Bob's. When I need a little advice about Saddam Hussein, I turn to country music.'

Natalie found the remote control and turned the TV off. I did not complain. 'Kuwait and Saudi Arabia are lucky to have the Sheriff to look after them,' Nat said.

I nodded.

'By the way, Steele, Ella Fitzgerald did not do *Strange Fruit*. That was Billie Holiday.'

'I sit corrected. Why didn't you tell me that before?'

'I was saving it up.'

I like being corrected by Nat and the Gooroo. Many Australians hate to admit they are wrong about anything. I think it is a national character flaw if there can be such a thing. Me, I like to learn something new every day and two things on Sunday.

THE Gulf War began on January 17, 1991, with an aerial bombardment of Iraq from Saudi Arabia and aircraft carriers in the Persian Gulf and Red Sea. American pilots and their allies flew more than 100,000 missions dropping 88,500 tonnes of bombs. That's a lot of freedom.

A popular song among American soldiers during the aerial and ground wars was *American Boy*.

" Winter "   Inspired by Vivaldi " Four seasons "

On the bank, beneath the ledge
And among the garden edge,
Colored azaleas are ablaze
Making bright the winter days.
Fairy flower of blooms and leaves of gold
Under the bush and tree,
Bringing warmth to a heart gone cold,
But refusing to get old.

At this site of beauty,
Grief recedes and hope return
To relive the time of spring
When the birds all be singing
And the breeze will be bringing
Sweet smell of flowers…
But….we are back at the beginning
Winter chills with all the trimmings.

Lillian E. Tebesceff (L. Ves-Te)

CATHY O'NEILL

SILENT KINGDOM
Anne Olsson

There is a journey you could take,
I suggest you take it soon.
For what you gain at journey's end
Is Life's most precious boon.

Open your unwilling eyes,
And watch the truth unfold,
And read within your deepest heart
The story yet untold.

Turn off the well-known track,
And wander deep within.
Here lies the peace and quiet joy
That is your nearest kin.

When you rest in innocence
And trust the gift of grace,
You'll find within the richest love,
In this most sacred place.

Do you doubt this precious peace?
Could this endless joy be real?
You'll find the answer in your soul,
And you'll find your place to heal.

'The kingdom lies within,' he said.
Thus spoke our gentle friend.
So trust these words and trust in grace,
And grace your life will mend.

A CLOSE ENCOUNTER

Ronald Holt

WHAT was that noise? It is coming from those thick bushes.

What is the matter with me? Am I getting spooked by an animal?

Maybe it was not such a good idea to take this shortcut home through the paddock at this late hour. Well it was a big night and I do have an early morning. It is a good night for a walk and besides the shortcut saves a lot of time at this hour.

The mist rising from the creek and the cloud partially covering the full moon does make for an eerie landscape. But don't be silly there is nobody around at this hour. It must be an animal.

I will just quicken my step and get away from it. I am not really scared but I can feel my pulse beginning to race and my anxiety rising.

That is odd, the faster I go, the closer and louder the noise becomes. I will stop and see what happens. The noise has stopped too. All I can hear are crickets. Am I imagining this? Am I only hearing my own footsteps echoing in bushes?

I know. It must be that neighbour of mine, McGillicudy, playing silly games. He has probably been out on the grog again. Turns him into a real idiot. Likes to play tricks on people.

'Hey, McGillicudy, I know it's you. Come out now! You're not funny!'

Hmm. Nothing. Maybe it isn't McGillicudy. I think I might just hurry on.

What is going on? The noise is getting closer. Lucky I have my pocket torch. It is not strong but I'll shine it towards the noise. Maybe it will scare any animals away.

What were those beady white flashes? Probably just the light in the eyes of the animal. The lights have disappeared. Perhaps I scared it away.

There is the noise again. I better get out of here. I think I will jog for a while.

My mind raced. Maybe it is an alien. Is this a close encounter of the third kind? Maybe I am going to be beamed up into a spaceship. No! Don't be silly. There are no such things as aliens. I hope.

The noise is getting louder. My heart is pounding like a drum and my pulse racing. Ouch, I trip on a broken branch. Oh, no, it is coming out of the bushes while I am down on the ground. How can I get away? I am doomed!

Beep. Beep. Beep.

What is that? It is my alarm clock. It can't be time to get up yet. I threw out my arm, fiddled for the off button pressing it to stop the beeping noise. It must have been a dream. It was so realistic I can still feel my heart pounding and sweat on my brow. I am not sure what I ate going to bed last night to cause a nightmare but I don't want any more dreams like that. That was the type of close encounter you can do without.

FANDRI'S EVENTFUL FIRST KISS

Kasper and Bailey Beaumont

'WATCH out for my crazy goat.'

Emina's voice was a bare whisper as she pulled Fandri by the shirt into the big wooden barn. The halflings could hear the sound of geese and ducks rustling in the straw and she closed the latch behind them. 'Old Billy Goat is very territorial and defends his barn with a passion.'

There was no sign of the recalcitrant goat while the brown-skinned halflings climbed the rickety staircase up to the musty loft. Their bond-fairies' glow lit up the gloom as they played chase above and around the hay bales, ignoring the eager teenagers.

Woodcutter's son and the resident scallywag of Southdale, Fandri had his first ever crush on this pretty shepherd's daughter. With her long brown hair and ever-present smile, Emina had won the hearts of many young lads in the village, but she only had eyes for fourteen-year-old Fandri.

'Kiss me, Fandri.' Emina's tone was almost pleading and she sat on a hay bale, beckoning her friend closer. She grabbed his shirt and pulled him down towards her, eyes shining with anticipation. Fandri stumbled in surprise and his knee grazed upon the rough-hewn floorboards, before he recovered and he was plonked down beside her.

'Just a minute, Emmy,' he protested. 'I'm not sure if I ought to be. . .' Whatever he had been trying to say was lost when Emina placed her finger on his lips.

'Shush.' She leaned her body against his, took her finger away and replaced it with soft pink lips that kissed him with passion.

Fandri was caught unawares, his heart thumping loudly in his chest. He stretched his arms forward to embrace her, but a sudden stabbing pain in his backside made him jump high into the air.

'M ... a ... a ... a,' bleated Billy Goat, tearing Fandri's cotton britches in two with his sharp horns.

'Help! Help!' Fandri bolted for the staircase and the red-eyed goat pursued him. Emina gave a frantic grab for the goat's collar, but wasn't fast enough to catch him before he clip-clopped down the stairs in pursuit of Fandri.

'Run Fandri! Billy's coming after you.'

He turned his head for a brief back glance as he ran around the door of the barn, shouting, 'I'm running all right.' He gave a yelp as the white goat rounded the corner of the barn and sprinted across the field towards him. Fandri spied the farmhouse, gathered the torn shreds of his pants and ran as fast as he could with the goat hot on his heels.

He ran in through the open kitchen door, slamming it shut behind him and heard the thud of the goat's horns bang into the wood. Luckily the door held strong and he sighed with relief. 'Mad goat!' His voice came out like a breathless pant in his explanation to Emina's mother.

Fandri and his wide-eyed fairy collapsed into a chair with heaving chests and pounding hearts.

Fandri-La closed her wings together to get a good look at her pert behind. 'That really hurt. I know that it was you Billy attacked, but it feels like my bottom is on fire.'

'Oh, you do make a fuss.' Emina's mother, Lyla, pointed a wooden spoon at the fairy. 'Why don't you heal your halfling and you'll feel better for it too?'

Fandri-La admitted that she was right and performed the healing ritual with Lyla-Li; singing soothing tunes and glowing from within while they spun in the air above the injured halfling.

Fandri smiled as the pain eased, until he looked through the open window to see Emina and her father striding purposefully across the field towards the farmhouse. Emina pulled on her father's arm and he was brusque when he shrugged her off. Hani was an overprotective parent of three pretty daughters and Fandri surmised that the red-faced farmer wasn't hurrying to enquire after his health.

'You were with a boy in the barn?' Hani's voice boomed across the field, sending chickens scurrying for cover from his big gumboots. Fandri shrank down below the windowsill, his knees feeling weak.

Lyla whispered in his ear. 'You'll be in for a whipping if he catches you, boy. Go hide in the cool room and I'll let you out when he's gone.' She handed Fandri a piping hot bread roll and bustled him into the cellar. Fandri-La followed with wide eyes.

The door had just closed when Hani burst into the kitchen. 'Where's that troublemaking boy?'

'Hani, leave the boy alone. I'm sure he's out in the fields somewhere.' Lyla sprinkled flour on a lump of dough and proceeded to knead it, avoiding eye contact with her fuming husband. 'I think your goat has made a new hole in the fence. Why don't you go check the boundaries?'

Hani harrumphed in reply and pulled the belt from his waist, jerking it so hard, it cracked like a whip. He turned on his heel and slammed the farmhouse door.

As Hani scoured the fields, Lyla bustled Fandri out of the cellar and through the back door of the house. The youngster looked nervously both ways before bolting towards the woods where he lived. The tall wheat grass gave way to the leafy coolness of the forest. Birds and small creatures scattered out of the path of Fandri and his fairy, who sprinted as fast as they could go.

After a furious burst of speed, Fandri slowed to a walk, relieved that the ordeal was over. He had frequent glances over his shoulder as his fairy stooped to drink nectar from the flowers.

A family of rabbits darted through the undergrowth, long ears twitching at the halfling's footstep. Ever the opportunistic hunter, Fandri grabbed a slingshot from his belt and rapidly shot pebble after pebble into the grass. A reassuring thump signalled a successful hit. Fandri dashed over to collect his prize and gave it a quick twist of the neck to alleviate suffering. He tied a string around the neck and slung it over his shoulder.

With a whisper of her tiny wings, Fandri-La flew down to whisper in the rabbit's ear and pat its head as it passed. She was saddened at the loss of life, but understood that Fandri never killed more than he could use or sell in the town.

Fandri patted the opening in his behind where the wind blew through the hole in his britches. 'Let's hurry home and get my spare trousers, Fandy. I doubt Ma will believe I ripped them on berry prickles.'

His fairy nodded with a tinkle of her bell. 'You do seem to attract trouble like a troll attracts flies. Not that we have ever seen a troll, of course.'

The halfling sighed. 'I promise you we will escape this village and see the world one day, little fairy. You and I were meant for bigger things than this boring old place.'

'I'd be happy with you anywhere.' Fandri-La smiled sweetly and flitted up to weave through the branches high above. She honestly seemed to enjoy her halfling's adventure-prone adolescence.

Their home came into view on the far side of a clearing. The robust log hut had been built here in the woods long before the small village of Southdale nearby. A halfling home for dozens of generations, it was a simple one-room bungalow with an open window at each end and a kitchen tacked onto the back. Currently three generations of the family lived there: Fandri, his parents and his paternal grandparents.

'Come on fairy. Let's get on in and have a nice rest. I think I've had enough troubles for one day.' Fandri-La nodded her head and started off across the clearing.

The bushes next to Fandri rustled and the halfling froze in surprise.

'M ... a ... a ... a,' the shaggy goat bleated and charged towards the halfling.

Fandri picked up the shreds of his britches and sprinted for the cabin.

The goat lowered its head as it charged the halfling and lifted him off the ground with both horns and he flew in through the open front window.

Fandri squealed as he rolled onto the cabin floor. Placing his hands to his sore reddened backside, he sniffed the air. 'What is that awful smell?'

'Oh silly.' Fandri-La flitted down holding his nose. 'Don't you know all billy's wee on their beards. He has marked you now. He will always be waiting to challenge you, if you ever return to Hani's farm.'

Fandri groaned. 'Ugh, girls. I don't know if they are really worth all this trouble.'

INSPIRED BY the adventure tales of David and Leigh Eddings

THE QUIET NON-AMERICAN
Bakthi Ross

A gentle Soul,
Quietly spoken,
Proper English
And proper manners.

He moved away from his homeland.
Dare he lose his mother tongue?
Years went,
Literature changed,
But his classy language stayed with him.

He was an author,
Wrote literary novels.
He wrote day and night.
When he read his story,
There was a silence in the room.

His high standard of English,
That's what made them quiet.
They listened quietly.
Most immigrants looked up to him.
His class and aristocracy
Stood with him until the end

Africa to Australia,
Papua New Guinea to Fiji,
India to China,
His status was recognized,
When he spoke in that gentle manner

We were inspired by him
To write that proper English,
Even though our texting language
Taking over our text.

Lilian

THE AUTHORS

Bailey Beaumont is 13-years old and enjoys drama, karate, music and cupcakes. Bailey has twice had short stories published in the *Write for Fun* anthology and was short-listed in an Australia-wide primary school competition. Bailey enjoys providing ideas for the *Hunters of Reloria* fantasy series.

Kasper Beaumont is the author of the three *Hunters of Reloria* fantasy series novels and also a short story which was published in last year's anthology. Kasper takes great delight in watching her readers become immersed in her fantasy adventures.

Frank Beecher was a boy in England during World War II. He became an avid reader. Not only did it take him away from the lack of food but it provided an escape to the life of his dreams. At age 17, he migrated to Australia and at age 21 he married. Now 56 years later he wonders how they managed to have three children so different to one another. Perhaps it was by allowing them to be the persons of their choice, he says. Frank joined the Arana Writers' Group in 2013 to improve his creative writing.

Bernie Dowling is a Pine Rivers journalist and author. His books include fiction and non-fiction. His first novel, *Iraqi Icicle* introduced the neo-noir detective Steele Hill who returns in two stories for this anthology. Both stories are new to print though *Someone to Watch Over Me* is in the eBook *Naughty Nineties*, available at online retailers.

Jaidyn Griffin, 17, of Kallangur, attends Pine Rivers State High School in Strathpine. He has always had a passion for writing, and using it as a tool to describe the 'indescribable'. In the future he hopes to study as a television journalist at university and use these skills as the foundation for his career.

Kerry Hall grew up in rural NSW and in her childhood was surrounded by animals, fiction characters, stories and verse. Kerry's nursing melded into a distinguished academic career from the 1980s. It was on those poor souls in her lectures the third-generation writer fine-tuned her wicked nurse's sense of humour. For the past few years Kerry has been beta reading, critically evaluating novels of varied genres. Her novel *The Tales of Cerahya, Book one: Morphids* will be published later in 2015. Kerry resides in a quiet community in Tasmania.

Caitlyn Heathwood is a 17-year-old Pine Rivers State High School student who enjoys academic and physical pursuits. She loves to coach and play netball and assist in cattle work and farm maintenance. Chopping firewood and composing a piece of writing may seem like polar opposites but accomplishing a challenging task is always gratifying. Caitlyn hopes to teach, using her passion for all things biological to inspire a new generation.

Ronald Holt retired from the Queensland public sector in 2006 after more than forty years' service – the last 14 years in the Office of Fair Trading. He wrote numerous reports and departmental correspondence on a wide range of issues and is now applying those skills to his love of creative writing. He has edited four anthologies in 2007, 2009, 2011 and 2013 for the Arana Writers' Group. He has had short stories published on Anzac Cove and global warming.

Belinda Janz has written short stories, poetry and stories for children as well as assisting in writing a radio play. She has won short-story competitions and has been published in Australia and overseas in magazines and anthologies. Her other interests include sewing, craft work, ancient history studies, cooking, reading, spirituality, massage and helping people.

Mikael Koch is a 17-year old from Petrie. He is in Year 12 at Pine Rivers State High School and in his spare time likes to read books and play video games. He wrote the short story *The Long Road Back*, inspired by the poem *Dulce Et Decorum Est*, with the intention of confronting the difficult subject of PTSD and war in general by showing the experiences of one who suffered through war and came back a broken man.

David MacLaughlin began writing for a staff magazine when he came fourth from world-wide entries for a travel article. Writing took a back seat as David became active in choral and Celtic choirs and musical theatre. After that it was time to give writing its proper priority in things cultural. As a member of Arana Writers' Group, David has contributed to the group's anthologies with articles factual, humorous, some fiction and travel tales.

Kyla Milne is 12-years old and is very excited to have her writing published in this anthology. Kyla enjoys writing and has many hobbies including Irish dancing, in which she competes at a national level and has won many first places. Kyla is also enrolled in the musical school of excellence program at her high school. Kyla and Kasper Beaumont met through a shared love of fantasy books and they have enjoyed working together on this story.

Vera Murray was born in Allora, Queensland. She has been writing since her school days. She is a former Pine Rivers Shire Councillor. She has edited a magazine overseas. While running the Writer's Circle group in Pine Rivers, she edited and published three anthologies. Her book *Move Over James Bond and Other Stories* and her first novel *Leap Year: Blood Lust* were recently published. Her latest book *Move Over plus Humorous Verses* was released in 2014.

Anne Olsson is a remedial therapist living and working in Pine Rivers. She has been an enthusiastic actor on the amateur stage and, in recent years, an eager world traveller. Her poetry and articles have been published in newspapers and magazines.

R. William Penshorn has travelled the world but still calls Australia home. Now retired and still touring, he spent most of his working years involved in surveying and civil engineering projects. He has written several movie scripts. His interests include comic collecting, classic automobiles, rock 'n' roll, art, surfing, and, of course, writing. His Tonka Toys were on display in the Queensland Museum's *Collectorama*, which ended in March 2014.

Raelene Purtill has, in her imagination, a husband of more than 20 years, three teenage children and a suburban existence, north-west of Brisbane. In the real world, she writes. Short stories are her preferred medium although she has produced plays and poems. She is a member of two writing groups, Strathpine Writers Group and Vanguard Writers, a group formed following a course at the Queensland Writers' Centre. Her blog is raelenep.blogspot.com.au.

Bakthi Ross is a member of the Caboolture Writer's Link. She started writing because of a dream and has written many children's books. Her ebooks are available at www.appspublisher.com. A mother of two children, she lives at Morayfield in Moreton Bay Region.

Brenda Simcox-Hunt came to Australia from England as a teenager with her parents in 1952. She is widowed with five children and eight grandchildren. She has been writing for more than 10 years and has had stories and poems published by local publishers. She is working on a book of short stories, two novels and three children's books.

Lach Thompson is a 29 year-old man whose honesty gets him into trouble; that's why he likes spinning yarns because when it's fiction they are less inclined to sue. He's a journalist, a surfer, a poor cook and an awful salesman. He's loved by a few, hated by a handful and unknown to most. *Mick's Exodus* is his first attempt at writing non-fiction since he was a schoolboy. He hopes you don't hate it.

Kate Tomsett is a Year 12 student at Pine Rivers State High School and is one of the two school captains. Kate enjoys volleyball, dance, music, volunteering for the community and, most of all, travel. She has recently been to Nepal to work with orphans, people with disabilities, the homeless, lepers and the blind. Her experiences have inspired Kate to attain a medical degree and work in third-world countries.

THE ILLUSTRATORS

The Pine Rivers University of the Third Age (U3A) has art classes conducted by Tutor Lillian Tebesceff.

The advanced students exhibit each year at places such as Pine Rivers Art Gallery and Pine Rivers Historical Museum.

Their next exhibition in early 2016 is of the artists' reimagining classical book covers.

The artists have illustrated our poems and short stories, along with regular designer and artist Ken Armstrong and other book cover designers and one journalist.

The Illustrators are:

Ken Armstrong, artist, graphic designer

Ynne Black, book cover designer

Margaret Brown, third-year U3A art student

K P Carroll, Keith, third-year U3A art student

Sonia Cuckson, Master Class student

Joan Hall, third-year U3A art student

Sandra Healy, semi-professional Master Class student

John O'Connell, Master Class student

Cathryn O'Neill, third-year U3A art student

Cathy O'Neill pseudonym of Cathryn O'Neill

Di Osborne, third-year U3A art student

Glenn Roberts, journalist, amateur photographer

Kate Somerville, third-year U3A art student

Janet Stuart, published writer, third-year U3A art student

Troy Stoilkovski, book cover designer

Lillian Tebesceff, artist, tutor Tintart U3A academy

John Wright Master Class student

www.ingramcontent.com/pod-product-compliance
Lightning Source LLC
Chambersburg PA
CBHW070009260626
47159CB00005B/1736